Thanks for Telling Me, Emily

DEIRDRE MADDEN

ORCHARD BOOKS

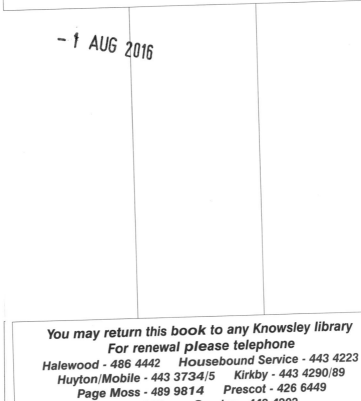

ORCHARD BOOKS
338 Euston Road, London NW1 3BH
Orchard Books Australia
Level 17-207 Kent Street, Sydney, NSW 2000, Australia
ISBN HB 978 1 84616 701 0
ISBN PB 978 1 84616 332 6
First published by Orchard Books in 2007
Paperback edition first published in 2008
Text © Deirdre Madden 2007
The right of Deirdre Madden to be identified as the author
of this work has been asserted by her in accordance with
the Copyright, Designs and Patents Act, 1988.
A CIP catalogue record for this book is
available from the British Library.
1 3 5 7 9 10 8 6 4 2 (HB)
5 7 9 10 8 6 4 (PB)
Printed in Great Britain
www.orchardbooks.co.uk

Orchard Books is a division of Hachette Children's Books

For Harry, with love

Contents

Gillnacurry

The story I am about to tell you took place in the little town of Gillnacurry, which was famous for being full of old and beautiful and remarkable things.

Just outside the town, for example, there was a very strange stone standing on the top of a hill. It was about the size of a small child and in the middle of the stone was a hole: a perfectly round hole. The stone had been put there thousands and thousands of years ago, and no one now had the foggiest idea why, or what it might be for. It did look rather pretty. The wind and rain had softened it and there was moss growing on it. But because it had been made before books and writing were invented, the people who put it there had left behind no explanation.

Brainy people came from all over the world to look at the holey stone. They scratched their heads and wondered about it, and then they went back to their own countries and wrote long, difficult books full of big words. They compared it to all the other holey stones in the world and they tried to guess what it was for. None of them ever suggested that perhaps the people who had put it there did so simply because they thought it might look nice standing in the middle of the field. The people of Gillnacurry loved the stone and were proud of it.

They were also proud of the church and its wonderful clock-tower, built of stout stone, that stood in the middle of the town square. It was also very old, but nothing like as old as the holey stone. Instead of being like this – 5, 6, 7 – the numbers on the clock face were like this – V, VI, VII. Above the face of the clock were two rather plump gold angels and above each of them again there was a row of little bells. The angel on the left was wearing a red sash and the one on the right a blue sash. They were holding sticks in their hands and when the clock struck the hour, the angels danced and rang the bells according to the time: three dings for three o'clock, six dings for six o'clock and so on. At twelve noon they also played a little tune and people would gather in the square below to watch them.

Gillnacurry also had an old, very fine castle, with everything a castle should have – turrets and towers, a moat and a drawbridge. It was very big, but for many years now nobody had lived in it and it looked rather sad and neglected. There was a weather vane on top of the tallest tower and instead of a rooster it was shaped like a long golden fish that turned and swung when the wind changed direction.

All the houses in the town were pretty. Some of them were large and grand and even the smallest houses were delightful. There were little cottages with thatched roofs and gardens full of lupins and roses; there were small stone houses with bright doors – yellow and blue and green – and twisted chimneys made of coloured brick.

Gillnacurry was also known for its fruit trees. In the spring one saw everywhere clouds of foamy blossom. In the autumn there were great baskets of fruit gathered in – crisp russet apples, moist juicy pears and succulent plums. And then in the winter...oh the winter was a most wonderful time to be in Gillnacurry! Because then they cooked and ate the fruit. There were jams and jellies, there were pear tarts and apples pies, there were all sort of scrumptious treats. If you know of a better place to be on a cold winter's night when the wind is howling around the rooftops than in a cottage in Gillnacurry, with a fire blazing in the grate and a plate of apple crumble and fresh cream in your hand, do please tell me where it is.

But the most remarkable thing of all about Gillnacurry was this. Every single house, be it large or small, grand or humble, had a pet animal of some kind. And the reason for this can be explained in three little words...

Emily's Pet Shop

Yes — Emily's pet shop. My story begins on a fine, sunny summer's morning and Emily was setting out for work. She lived in one of the nicest cottages in Gillnacurry, which is saying something. It was a tiny place with deep windows and it was completely covered in thick green ivy, so that it looked as if the cottage was wearing a woolly jumper that someone had knitted for it. This was a special day because although Emily lived alone, there was someone with her this morning: a little girl with blonde pigtails followed her out of the house.

'Good girl, Keira!' said Emily, beaming broadly. 'Let's get going, we don't want to be late.'

They climbed onto their bicycles and cycled through the town. Everyone knew and liked Emily and they waved as she passed. Some of the people they saw were walking their dogs, and the dogs all barked excitedly. Cats dozing on walls and windowsills perked up and mewed; some even hopped down and ran along beside the bikes for a little way. As they peddled along they could see the holey stone, high on its hill in the distance. They cycled down streets lined with apple trees, they whizzed past the big empty castle. Just as they arrived at the shop door, the hour hand on the town clock moved to IX, and the angel with the red sash rang his bell nine times.

Emily unlocked the door of the shop and

went in. 'Good morning my dears! Good morning!' she said.

'Good morning Emily!' all the animals cried, although of course it didn't sound like this. It sounded like a mad mixture of mews and wuffs and squeaks and squawks, but Emily knew what they meant to say. Some people thought Emily was a bit batty because she talked to animals, but she knew that the animals understood her. She knew that they liked to know what was happening and to have things explained to them. This morning she stood in the middle of the room and clapped her hands.

'Dear friends,' she said, 'before we begin today, I have something very important to tell you. Let me introduce my niece Keira, who is eight years old. Today is the first day of the school holidays. Keira has come to stay with me and she will be working with us for the whole summer. She loves animals and she's really looking forward to helping me look after you all.'

Keira felt her face go pink. She was aware of being stared at by quite a little crowd of creatures but she didn't like to stare back. She wasn't quite sure what to do, so she whispered, 'Hello' and gave a little bow. The animals seemed to like this, for there were more squeaks and squawks, but this time it was all very gentle, as if they knew she felt nervous and shy and wanted to reassure her. She could hear a cat purring and a dog made a soft, happy whimpering sound.

'Let me introduce you to everybody,' said Emily to Keira. 'This is Noreen the snake.'

Noreen was curled up in the bottom of her tank and kept very still. 'Tell me honestly now, are you afraid of snakes?'

'Maybe just a little bit,' said Keira in a small voice.

'That's probably just because you're not used to them,' said Emily soothingly. 'Once you get to know her, you'll love her. She's a most delightful animal. Now this,' she went on, scooping up a large furry cat from its basket, 'is Mulvey. Say hello to Keira, Mulvey,' and the cat purred louder than ever.

'He's lovely,' said Keira, stroking him between his pointed, chocolate-coloured ears.

'Now as you can see,' Emily continued as she gently replaced Mulvey in his basket, 'we also have four white mice. Their names are Milly, Tilly, Billy and Willy.'

'Gosh, how can you tell them apart?' said Keira, looking at the squirming tangle of white fur and tiny paws, twitching snouts and glistening whiskers. 'They all look exactly the same to me.' At that she thought she heard Mulvey snigger, but when she looked at him he was sitting up washing his face, and seemed to be paying no attention whatsoever to what they were saying.

'It is difficult,' Emily admitted, picking up one of the mice. 'If I take the time and look at them very closely, then I know which is which, but when they're all together and moving fast, you can't be sure.'

'And do they get on well with the cat?'

'Oh yes, Mulvey loves them. All the animals get on well together.'

Keira glanced again at the cat and this time it gave her a winning smile. Keira giggled and the cat winked, curled up, and pretended to be asleep.

'What a wonderful pet shop,' the little girl thought. 'This is going to be the most marvellous summer!'

Sitting on a perch near the cat was a magnificent parrot, with red, green, blue and yellow feathers. 'That's Captain Cockle,' said Emily seeing Keira looking at him. 'Goodness me, Bubbles, do be quiet! Calm down!' she went on.

Bubbles was a Yorkshire Terrier, a tiny little scrap of a dog, so small that when she barked, as she was doing now, she lifted herself off the ground and seemed to bounce up and down. There was also a hamster called Betty who was running on a wheel. Keira was beginning to get confused, there were so many animals. Was Bubbles the dog and Betty the hamster or was it the other way around? Emily reminded her which was which. 'Don't worry, you'll remember them all soon. But it's time we started giving them their breakfasts, I'm sure they're all terribly hungry.'

In the next two hours there wasn't a minute to spare, as they put out milk and food and water, then washed up the empty bowls and plates. They cleared out the litter trays and gave the mice and the hamster clean straw. It's very nice to have pets but you have to work hard to look after them properly, and Keira was tired when eleven o'clock came.

'Time for us now,' said Emily, putting out two glasses of milk and a plate of chocolate biscuits. When they had finished their elevenses, Keira took Bubbles for a walk to the holey stone. How the little dog barked and bounced with delight when Emily clipped on the lead! 'This is something I'll want you to do every day,' Emily said to Keira.

The child and the dog both enjoyed being out for a while in the bright summer sunshine. Bubbles tugged and pulled on the lead as she scampered along beside Keira, and from the top of the hill they could see the whole town of Gillnacurry spread out below them, with its orchards and coloured houses.

When they got back to the shop there was a steady stream of customers. Emily sold mountains of pet-food: bags of birdseed, nuts, dog-biscuits and cat food. She also sold special shoulder bags for carrying cats and small dogs, with a little hole in the corner so that the animal's head could peek out. She sold baskets and rugs and cages, toy mice and rubber bones. But Keira noticed something rather odd – she didn't seem to sell any animals. When she asked her aunt about this, Emily gave a strange smile. 'I do sometimes,' she said, 'but not very often. Pretty well everyone in

Gillnacurry has an animal by now. And that suits me fine!'

In the early afternoon, Emily said to Keira, 'Would you like to say hello to Noreen?' They crossed to the tank where the snake was lying very still.

'Hello Noreen.'

'Would you like to touch her?' Keira shook her head.

'Do you think she'll bite you?'

'No.'

'Do you think she'll feel all horrible and slimy, is that it?'

'Yes,' said Keira in a very small voice.

'She doesn't, you know. Lots of people think that but she's actually nice and smooth and warm. Believe it or not, she feels just like a handbag.' Emily bent over the tank and stroked Noreen with the tip of her finger. The snake uncoiled a little. 'Show us your tongue, there's a good girl,' she said and to Keira's amazement, a little black forked tongue flickered out of Noreen's jaws and was gone again.

'Do I have to touch her?' Keira asked.

'Of course not,' said Emily, 'not if you don't want to.'

Just at that moment, a huge great lorry pulled up outside and Emily gave a big smile.

'Why, look who's here!'

Finbarr

The lorry was painted dark blue and it said on the side in yellow letters

FINBARR'S FEEDS

for your animal's needs.

A tall skinny man got out of the cab of the lorry and *clang!* came into the shop. He had a great big soppy grin on his face and was carrying a basket with a lid on it. 'Hello Emily!'

'Hello Finbarr. How are you? This is my niece Keira. She's going to be working with me for the school holidays.'

'Are you, Keira? Oh that'll be lovely,' said Finbarr, and his eyes grew very big. 'That'll be really nice for you, seeing Emily every single day in the week for the whole summer.' He beamed down at Emily who, unlike Finbarr, was rather short. Keira smiled and nodded.

'Finbarr brings all the food for the animals to the shop,' Emily said.

'Is that what's in the hamper?' Keira asked.

'Goodness no, all the food's out in the lorry,' said Emily. 'Why don't you show her what you've got there, Finbarr?'

Finbarr lifted up the lid very gently and Keira peered into the hamper. Curled up inside were two marmalade kittens.

'Oh, aren't they beautiful!' she cried.

'I bring the pets as well as the pet food,' Finbarr said. 'Emily tells me what she needs and I get it for her.'

'We'll put these two in with Mulvey,' said Emily. 'He'll look after them until such time as they find new owners.' She gently lifted the first kitten out of the basket. Its eyes grew wide with fright but Emily stroked it and spoke to it soothingly. She set it in beside the older cat, and for a few moments Mulvey and the kitten stared at each other. Then, slowly and carefully, the big furry cat started to wash the new arrival. He licked the top of the kitten's head and it staggered, almost fell over, but Mulvey kept going as Keira lifted the second little ball of orange fur in beside them.

By the time Finbarr had carried in all the pet food from the back of the lorry and stored it away for Emily, Mulvey had washed both kittens from the tips of their pointed ears to the soft pink pads on the soles of their feet. Keira gave them a saucer of milk. She thought that Mulvey, being so much bigger and stronger, might push them out of the way and drink it all himself. She was astonished to see that the older cat did nothing of the kind, but sat back with his paws folded, watching as the two kittens lapped the saucer empty and clean.

'I suppose I'd best be off then. I'll see you on Friday,' Finbarr said. 'Anything special you'll be needing?'

Emily asked him to bring a tank of tropical fish and a rabbit. The whole time he had been working, she had noticed that there was something strange about Finbarr, but she couldn't quite work out what it was. He looked sort of lopsided today. She stared at him now and he stared back at her, still with a great, big, soppy grin on his face. Suddenly she realised what the problem was. 'Finbarr, you've got your cardigan buttoned up all wrong. You've got a button left over at the top and a buttonhole left over at the bottom.'

Finbarr gawped down at his front. 'Have I? Ooh, thanks for telling me, Emily!'

Night Creatures

It was midnight in Gillnacurry. The hands of the town clock moved to XII and the two angels with their coloured sashes played their tune on the bells. Light from a street lamp shone softly through the window of Emily's pet shop, where not all the animals were asleep.

'What a nice little girl Keira is!' said Bubbles.

'Yes,' said Noreen. 'I'm really sorry that she's afraid of me.'

'No wonder, great big poisonous snake like

you. Scary looking, you are.' This was Mulvey, of course, and Noreen was just about to reply when Captain Cockle cut in.

'Pay no heed to him. You know what a tease he is.'

Mulvey laughed at this. He had a great big loud guffaw of a laugh as do all cats, although they always take great care not to laugh around people. At the very most you might hear one give a little snigger now and then, although even that is rare. But at night when there was no one around except for the other animals, Mulvey laughed loud and long. Bubbles found herself laughing too, and Captain Cockle and even Noreen couldn't help smiling.

'Bet you anything that before the week's out she'll have touched you, Noreen,' said Bubbles. 'Bet she says "Isn't she lovely? She feels nice and warm. SHE'S JUST LIKE A HANDBAG!"' All the animals who were still awake, including Noreen, chorused this last sentence together, for they had heard it so many times they thought it was hilarious. People always said exactly the same thing when they finally plucked up the courage to touch Noreen.

Click! Click! Click! Betty the hamster was still running on her wheel.

'You can stop that now,' said Mulvey. 'You're making me tired looking at you. Why do you do it anyway? Are you trying to keep your weight down?'

Again all the animals laughed at this, for Betty was a roly-poly little beastie, like all hamsters.

'And what about you lot, eh?' Mulvey was staring down into the basket where the white mice lived. They all scrambled and ran when they saw his big face leaning over them, but he put in a paw and scooped one of them up.

'Hello Tilly. Or is it Milly? Emily's right, you know, it's really hard to tell you apart.' By now the mouse was dangling by its tail. 'Put me down, you big bully! Put me down!'

Mulvey gave another great belly laugh but

he carefully lowered the mouse back in with its companions.

Mulvey was an extraordinary looking cat, enormously furry so that he seemed very big, but when you picked him up you could feel that his body was actually quite small under all the fur. He was a creamy colour, like coffee made on milk, except for his ears, his paws and his nose, which were the colour of dark chocolate. I say 'nose' but one of the strange things about him was that he could hardly be said to have a nose. When you looked at Mulvey sideways his face was completely flat, something the other animals never mentioned because they knew he found it slightly embarrassing. He did have wonderful eyes, though. As blue as sapphires and perfectly round, they more than made up for the want of a nose. A splendid set of whiskers finished him off so that Mulvey was as magnificent a pussycat as you are ever likely to see.

Just at that he heard a little mewing sound

coming from the cat basket. 'Hello Tiger! What's your name then?'

'I'm Alexander,' said the kitten, 'and this is my brother Aloysius. I know they're rather big names for such small cats,' he went on apologetically, 'but our mother told us we'd grow into them.'

'Your mum,' Mulvey replied, 'is one smart tabby. It's all very well being called something like Twinkle or Buttercup when you're little, but when you grow up, it's another story. I've known cats, fine great big tom-cats, that had their lives ruined because they were given cute names when they were kittens. Your mum is absolutely right.'

'Where are we? What's going to happen to us?' asked Aloysius.

'You're in the best pet shop in the whole wide world,' said Mulvey comfortably. 'You'll stay here for a while and I'll look after you. Not that you'll need looking after, 'cos Emily's so good to us all but if anything's worrying you, you come straight to old Mulvey, do you hear? And then one day, maybe in a week, maybe in a few months, someone will come in and buy you – both of you, 'cos Emily doesn't split up animals that arrive together. She knows everybody in this town and she'll make sure you go to a good home.

'One important thing though!' And he bent down, whispered in the kittens' ears. 'No teasing the mice! That's my job and, in any case, they know I don't mean it. They know I'm a big old softy and I wouldn't hurt a fly, but two tigers like you – brrr! You'd frighten the life out of them, soon as wink.' The two tiny kittens were pleased to hear this and they promised that they would leave the mice alone.

'What if someone buys you before they buy us?' asked one of the kittens.

'I don't think there's much chance of that,' said Mulvey. 'Me and Bubbles and Noreen and Captain Cockle, we've been here for years and years now. I don't think Emily wants to sell us. Anyway, you should get some sleep, you've had a long day. Fancy something to eat before I tuck you in? You can have some of my cat treats if you want.'

The animals were always fed last thing before the shop closed every evening. Mulvey usually got a heap of tiny fishy biscuits and he gobbled them down in a twinkling, but this evening he had left them untouched, while the kittens ate theirs. 'Help yourselves,' he said, nodding to the full bowl.

'Are you sure?' asked the kittens.

The big cat nodded.

'Thanks, Mulvey! You're a star!'

All the animals watched as the kittens crunched their way through the cat treats. They knew how much Mulvey loved his grub and how hungry he must be, but he didn't show it. Even the mice looked at him with affection and thought what a big, kind, gentle, softy he was.

Friday with Finbarr

Finbarr was a tall, skinny fellow and he lived in a tall, skinny house. Every room was on a different storey. The kitchen was on the ground floor, the dining room was above that, the sitting room above that, the bedroom above that, and at the very top of the house was the bathroom. (He also had a loo downstairs in the hall, because it would have been very inconvenient otherwise.) He slept well every night because even if he wasn't tired at the end of the day, by the time he had climbed all the stairs to his bedroom he would always be worn out, and only too happy to put on his pyjamas and go to sleep.

On the table beside his bed was an alarm clock with two brass bells on it. On that Friday morning at seven-thirty sharp, they jangled loudly. Finbarr dozily put his hand out from under the blankets and turned the clock off. 'I'mgoingtoseeEmilytoday' was his first sleepy thought. 'I'mgoingtoseeEmilytodayI'mgoing toseeEmilytodayI'mgoingtoseeEmilytoday.' And then suddenly his brain switched on and he realised the meaning of what he was thinking. He shot up in the bed with his hair on end and his eyes as wide as if he had just seen a ghost and he shouted aloud, 'I'M GOING TO SEE EMILY TODAY!'

After that it was all go. He fell onto the floor, and stumbled into the bathroom, and got washed and dressed in record time. He was so excited about the thought of seeing Emily that he put his jumper on inside out and didn't even realise it. Then he went downstairs, down and down and down to the kitchen to make his breakfast.

'Maybe she'll be wearing her blue dress,' he thought as he put three large spoonfuls of tea in the coffee machine. 'She looks lovely in her blue dress. But she's got a pink skirt and cardigan and she looks nice in that too.' He poured orange juice all over his cornflakes and ate them dreamily as he thought about Emily, trying to decide which of the two outfits suited her best. 'Blue goes with her eyes,' he thought, spreading butter and marmalade thickly on what he thought was a piece of toast but which was actually a wicker table mat. 'I've never seen anybody with such beautiful blue eyes as Emily.' He drank the weird brown liquid that came out of the coffee machine and he chomped his way through most of the table mat.

Sitting in the middle of the kitchen table was

a tank full of tropical fish. 'Soon you'll be in Emily's pet shop, my beauties,' he said, tapping on the glass of the tank with his finger. The fish seemed to pay him no heed. They looked like shreds and scraps of coloured silk or velvet, and they swam on peacefully.

Breakfast over, he put the fish tank in the lorry and collected a heavy white rabbit from the hutch in the back garden where it had spent the night. Finbarr put it in the same basket he had used to deliver the kittens earlier in the week and gave it a carrot to keep it happy. He had loaded up the lorry with pet food the night before and so, in no time at all, he was ready for the road.

She wasn't wearing her blue dress and she wasn't wearing her pink skirt and cardigan either. Today Emily was wearing a dress Finbarr had never seen before. It was pale green and it was printed all over with daisies. It was nicer by far than either the blue dress or the pink skirt and cardigan. Finbarr stood there in the middle of the floor with a fish tank cradled in his right arm and a basket, with a rabbit's nose poking out from under the lid, dangling from his left hand. His mouth was hanging open and for a few minutes he couldn't speak. 'I like the frock, Emily,' he whispered at last.

'Thank you, Finbarr,' she said brightly. 'It's new. Keira helped me choose it. You can put the tank of fish over on the table please. Now, who have we here?' and she lifted the lid on the basket.

'He used to belong to a magician,' Finbarr explained as Emily lifted out an enormous white rabbit. 'There were doves too, and a lady in a spangly outfit. The magician used to saw her in half every evening. Then they decided to get married and go and live in the country. She wanted to keep the doves, but she didn't like the rabbit. So I heard about it and I said I knew you could find him a good home.'

'I'm glad you did. Silly woman in her

spangly outfit,' Emily whispered into one of the rabbit's long white ears. 'Who wouldn't want a lovely fellow like you?' The rabbit's pink nose twitched in delight. Finbarr stared mournfully at them as if he'd have given anything to be a rabbit himself and to have Emily whisper in his ear, 'Who wouldn't want a lovely fellow like you?'

When he had carried in all the food for the animals from the lorry he said to Emily, 'I heard a rumour that the castle has been sold. They say a rich woman has bought it and she's coming to live here with her little son. I think it must be true because when I was driving past this morning, there was someone up on the roof polishing the big gold fish.'

'Well, if it is true I'm sure she'll be very happy here. Everybody likes Gillnacurry.'

There was no reason for Finbarr not to go but still he wanted to stay. He was standing right beside Noreen's tank so he said to Keira, 'Grand snake, isn't it?'

'Yes. I was a little bit afraid of her when I arrived but now that I've been here for a while I think she's very nice.'

'But you still haven't been able to touch her yet, have you?' said Emily.

'No.'

'Why don't you give it a try now?'

Keira went over and stood beside Finbarr, and peered into the tank. Noreen really was a spectacular snake, black with a big gold zigzag running the whole length of her body. 'Hello Noreen,' Keira said. Noreen lay as still as a stone. Keira put her hand in and stroked the snake very gently. 'Why she's lovely!' she cried. 'She feels all warm and smooth. She's just like a handbag!'

As soon as Keira said this something very odd indeed happened. Every single animal in the shop, except for the rabbit and the tropical fish, made a funny noise. It was a kind of a mad gurgle, a mixture of squeaks and squawks that burst from them and that they all tried to swallow. If you didn't know anything about animals you would have thought that they had all burst out laughing but immediately tried to hide it. Keira was sure, absolutely sure, that she heard a snigger from Mulvey's basket and even Noreen appeared to be smiling.

Emily looked puzzled. 'Whatever is the matter with you all?' she said, but all the animals just sat there, silent now, and stared at her.

'Suppose I'd best be off,' Finbarr said. 'Goodbye Keira. See you soon, Emily.'

'Cheerio. Oh and by the way, Finbarr,'

'Yes?'

'You have your jumper on inside out. I can see the seams and the label.'

'Have I?' he said. 'Have I really? Ooh, thanks for telling me, Emily!'

Presto's Secrets

Late that night Finbarr lay down in his long, skinny bed in his tall, skinny house, hoping for sweet dreams of Emily. Little did he know that over in the pet shop all the animals were talking about him.

'He's potty about her,' said Captain Cockle. 'Completely potty.'

'He looks like this when he sees Emily,' said Bubbles and she stood in the middle of the floor with a dopey look on her face and her mouth hanging open. Now that there was no one around to hear them, they didn't try to conceal their laughter, with Mulvey's big belly-laugh loudest of all.

'You should have seen him at breakfast this morning,' said one of the tropical fish. She told them about Finbarr putting orange juice on his cornflakes and eating the table mat, and all the animals laughed until they wept, until they pleaded with the fish not to tell them any more because their sides were sore from laughing so much.

'It's Emily, though, who's really being silly,' said Bubbles eventually, as she wiped her eyes with a final chuckle. 'How can she not see that he's dotty about her?'

'I think she's too busy looking after us,' said Noreen. 'She never thinks about herself and what might be good for her.'

'You're lucky that woman in the spangly outfit didn't want you,' said Mulvey to the rabbit. 'You're better off here with us. Isn't that right, lads?' The two marmalade kittens nodded. They had settled in well and were as happy as could be. They now had their very own basket, and a tartan rug, just like Mulvey's. 'Anyway you haven't even told us your name yet.'

'Presto,' said the rabbit. 'As in "Hey Presto!"'

'And what was it like being in a magic show?'

Presto said that it had been a bit boring, because he was always the last trick of the night and he used to get fed up waiting. He said the show was exciting the first time you saw it, but when you saw it hundreds and hundreds of times and you knew how all the magic was done then it just wasn't the same. But none of the other animals had ever been to a magic show, so they were fascinated by everything Presto told them.

The magician was called Mister Marvel and his assistant, the woman in the spangly outfit who didn't like rabbits, was called The Beautiful Esmeralda.

'Her real name was Doris Crump and she wasn't a bit beautiful; Emily's much prettier. Mister Marvel used to put her in a box every evening and cut her in two. He'd wheel the top half of her to the right-hand side of the stage and the bottom half of her over to the left. She was still able to wriggle her toes and to smile.' All the animals gasped in amazement when they heard this. 'He used to make doves appear out of coloured silk handkerchiefs and he used to pull me out of an empty top hat. It was a good show,' said Presto, remembering it all now. 'Everybody liked it.'

'And did I hear you say that you knew how all the tricks were done?' said Mulvey.

The rabbit nodded.

The cat smiled. 'Bet you don't.'

'Oh yes I do!' said Presto.

'Don't believe you.'

'I know everything there is to know about magic.'

'Why don't you tell me then,' said Mulvey smoothly. And to his surprise, the rabbit fell for it. 'Well, so long as you don't tell anybody else. Now listen carefully.' He put his mouth up close to the cat's pointed ear and spoke to him very quietly for a good quarter of an hour.

'Now do you believe me?' said the rabbit when it had finished. Mulvey nodded, made a dopey face.

'Oooh, thanks for telling me, Presto!'

'And how are you all this evening?' he went on, strolling over to the white mice and pulling one of them out as usual. 'Hello darling! You look...delicious! I mean beautiful! Beautiful!' But it was too late. The poor little mouse had fainted in fright and lay there out cold on the flat of Mulvey's paw with his four tiny legs straight up in the air. The cat carefully put him back in with the other mice, sprinkled his snout with water from their drinking bowl to wake him up again. 'Silly, Billy, Willy, Milly or Tilly,' said the cat as the little mouse staggered to its feet. 'I was only teasing, you know.'

'Don't do that ever again!' cried the mouse angrily.

'Really, some people!' sighed Mulvey. 'No sense of humour at all.'

Click! Click! Click! He went over to where Betty was running on the spot. 'Hold on tight!' The cat put his paw to the wheel, stopped it, and then spun it in the opposite direction. The hamster gripped the wire rungs tightly and flattened her plump body against the wheel as she spun backwards, upside down, whirling and spinning, looping the loop and shrieking with delight. 'Yippee! Do it again, Mulvey! This is great fun! Oh please, again, again! Wheeeeeeeeeeee!' Round and round and round she went.

All the animals laughed, even the mice for

no matter how mischievous he was, it was impossible to be cross with Mulvey for long.

What none of them would ever have believed was that the very next day, something awful was going to happen that would put an end to their happy days and nights together.

Henrietta

The following day began much like any other. Emily and Keira opened the shop and fed the animals. Keira took Bubbles for a walk and by the time she got back, Finbarr was there, staring dreamily at Emily as she prepared some mid-morning milk and biscuits for all three of them. Finbarr had brought along three new guinea pigs and to settle them in he was sitting quietly with one on his lap and the other two on his shoulders when *clang!* the door of the shop opened. A woman came in, accompanied by a small boy.

She was quite a strange looking person. Her eyes were completely round, like Mulvey's, and she had drawn a black line around each of them, which made them look even rounder. She was wearing a heap of shawls and scarves; and many silver bracelets, that tinkled when she moved. 'My name,' said the woman with an air of great importance, 'is Henrietta Fysshe-Pye. Two y's, two e's, two s's and a hyphen.' All the creatures in the shop made that strange gurgling, snurfling noise of animal laughter being swallowed, and Keira almost giggled out loud. 'And this is my son, Ryan. Say hello, Ryan.'

'Hello,' he said, in so tiny a voice he could hardly be heard.

'Hello Ryan. Hello Missus. I'm Finbarr Frizell. Two f's, a z, no hyphens and a load of other letters but I can't remember what they are right now. That's my van outside,' and he pointed to it. '"Finbarr's Feeds, for your animal's needs." And this is Emily and Keira. It's Emily's shop, the best pet shop in the whole world!'

Henrietta stared at him as if she thought he was completely weird, but clearly didn't consider it was worth her while replying to this tall, skinny fellow covered in guinea pigs. Instead she turned to Emily and said, 'I've just bought Gillnacurry Castle. It was hugely expensive but that's not a problem to me because I've got pots of money. My father invented salt and vinegar crisps, and every time somebody buys a packet of them, part of the money goes to me. Ryan didn't want to come and live here. He didn't want to leave his friends, the silly boy. But I said he could have a pet to make up for it, didn't I, Ryan?'

'Yes,' the boy replied, in the same tiny little voice.

'Now, what would you like?'

'The marmalade kittens are wonde—'

'No, no,' said Henrietta before he could finish. 'They'll only grow up to be big fat ginger toms and I'm not having that sort of thing in my castle.'

'But they're gorgeous, and they've got stripes on their tails and even on their tummies.'

'Ryan, did you hear me? No ginger toms!'

'What about this beautiful white rabbit?' Emily said, pointing at Presto.

'I don't like rabbits,' said Henrietta. 'They look stupid. I don't like the way their noses twitch all the time. I mean, what's the point? What are they trying to prove?'

'Emily was asking Ryan, not you,' said Finbarr.

'I'd love a rabbit,' the little boy whispered.

'Well, you're not getting one,' said Henrietta, and she glared at Finbarr.

She started to walk around the shop, trailing her scarves and shawls and tinkling all her silver bracelets. 'Hmm, the parrot isn't bad,' she said, peering up at Captain Cockle, high on his perch.

'I'm not sure that he's for sale,' said Emily.

'Not for sale? What sort of a pet shop is it if all the little beasties aren't for sale?'

Emily didn't know what to say to this. Over the years she had grown so fond of some of the animals that she always managed to talk people out of buying her favourites, and persuaded them to choose something else instead.

Henrietta had arrived at Mulvey's basket. She stared down at him with her perfectly round eyes, and Mulvey stared brazenly back with his. 'Nicer colour than the other cats,' she said, and then gave a loud shriek of laughter as he turned his head away. 'It's got no nose! Can you believe it? Come and look at this, Ryan, this is hilarious! Its face is completely flat. Have you ever seen a cat with no nose before?'

Keira was aware of a terrible hush falling over the whole shop. None of the animals could believe what they were hearing. That someone could be so rude! Mulvey remained sitting completely still with his head turned away, but the very end of his tail began to slowly twitch back and forth. The other animals knew this was a bad sign. They knew this only ever happened when he was furious.

'I think that's what that kind of cat's supposed to look like, Mummy. Their heads are a different shape to ordinary cats.'

'Well I think it's a hoot!'

And then Henrietta spotted Noreen.

'AAAAARGH! IT'S A SNAKE! A HORRIBLE, BIG, FAT POISONOUS SNAKE! HELP! HELP!' She screeched so loud and so long that she terrified poor Noreen, who had actually been fast asleep. Noreen shot out of her coils; darted across the bottom of her tank in fear. This only made Henrietta scream even louder. 'EEEEEEK! IT'S TRYING TO GET OUT OF THE TANK! IT WANTS TO BITE ME! SLIMY REVOLTING BEAST! YEURGH!'

'Noreen won't hurt you,' Keira said gently, trying to calm down Henrietta. 'She's a very nice snake, and she isn't a bit slimy. I used to think that too, but I was wrong. If you touch her you'll see, she's just like a handbag.'

'Are you mad, little girl? Are you quite, quite mad? Touch a snake? Touch that horrible, nasty thing?' She pointed at Bubbles and said to Emily, 'I'll take the little dog, the parrot and the cat. Any chance of a discount because it has no nose? Do you deliver?'

'Do we deliver?' Emily said faintly. It was turning out to be such a strange and upsetting morning that she no longer knew.

'Any delivering has to be done round here, I do it,' said Finbarr. The guinea pig that had been sitting on his shoulder was now on the top of his head. 'And you listen to me, Mrs Meat-Pie...'

'Fysshe!' shrieked Henrietta. 'Fysshe! Not Meat-Pie, Fysshe-Pye! Two y's, two e's, two s's and a hyphen.'

'Whatever,' said Finbarr who was getting desperately confused. 'I'll bring the animals round to you tomorrow morning, and you'd better be good to them because they're used to being loved.'

Henrietta scribbled a cheque for the amount that Emily requested and handed it over. 'Come along, Ryan,' she said, 'let's get out of here. I don't believe that this is the best pet shop in the world, but it's certainly the craziest.'

The Last Night

The animals could hardly believe that this would be their last night together. Never again would they all sit listening to the angels on the clock playing their midnight tune and then settle down to discuss all the day's events. Never again would they hear Mulvey's great belly-laugh, nor see Bubbles lift herself clean off the ground when she barked, nor Captain Cockle nibble his fresh pineapple and stand on one leg.

The cat tried to put a brave face on things and went over to the white mice, lifted one of them out onto his paw. But neither of them had the heart for the usual games. 'Mulvey,' said the little mouse staring up into the big furry face, 'we know you didn't mean all the things you used to say to us. We know you were only teasing. You might find this hard to believe but we'll miss you terribly.'

The cat smiled sadly. 'I'll miss you too, Billy. And you Milly, and Tilly and Willy,' he went on, pointing to each in turn.

The mice were astounded. 'So you can tell us apart!'

Mulvey smiled again, only this time it was more of a mischievous grin. ''Course I can tell you apart! Didn't you say yourself, you knew I was only teasing?'

There was a strange silence in the shop tonight. The familiar *Click! Click! Click!* of Betty's wheel was missing because she was too upset to do any running. Instead, she simply sat there with her snout buried in her paws.

'Come on Betty my love, you'll get fat if you don't keep up with the old exercise. You'll lose your figure.'

The hamster took her paws away and said, 'I can't. Not tonight, Mulvey, I just can't.'

The cat was moved to see that her eyes were full of tears.

'Oh this is dreadful, just dreadful!' exclaimed Bubbles all of a sudden. 'I know that by this time tomorrow, Mulvey and Captain Cockle and I will all be in a castle but I just want to be here. I can't bear to think that this is the end.'

'Remember that it could be worse,' said Noreen. 'At least the three of you will all be going. You can stick together and look out for each other. Just think, if this woman had only wanted one pet then one of us would have had to go it alone.'

This was so lonely and horrible a thought that the animals were shocked even to imagine it. Betty began to sob, but Captain Cockle said stoutly, 'Noreen's right. We'll help each other through this.'

'Mulvey,' said a small voice, 'we saved these for you.' It was Aloysius, one of the marmalade kittens and he was sitting beside a double helping of cat treats. 'You can eat them now if you like, or you can take them with you tomorrow, in case you get hungry on the way to the castle,' he said.

The big cat hardly knew what to reply to this, he was so touched. 'Thanks, lads,' he said at last. 'It helps to know that I won't be the last cat in the shop. It's good to know that you'll be here. I'll be thinking of you and I'm counting on you to keep up the good work.'

'We will,' promised Alexander. 'We'll tease the mice for you, but we'll never harm them. I wish we could go instead of you. The little boy wanted us and he seemed nice. It could be fun to live in a castle.'

'I wish I was going too,' said Presto mournfully. 'It wouldn't bother me at all for

I've only been here for a day or so, and when I was in the magic show I was used to moving around all the time. I was used to grumpy women too,' he added, thinking of 'The Beautiful Esmeralda'. 'If you can put up with Doris Crump, you can put up with anybody.'

'Nobody has gone anywhere yet,' said Noreen, 'and I have a plan that just might work. Presto, we'll need your help. Now, gather round all of you and listen carefully.'

The Following Morning

When Finbarr arrived the following morning to take the animals to the castle, Emily didn't even notice that he was wearing one blue sock and one green one, so she didn't point it out to him and he didn't say, 'Ooh, thanks for telling me, Emily!' as would have happened on any ordinary day. Instead, the whole shop, usually so happy and calm, was in total uproar. Captain Cockle was flying around squawking, and refused to land on his perch, no matter how many pieces of mango Keira waved to coax him down. Mulvey was sitting on a high shelf up near the ceiling and wouldn't budge. And as for Bubbles...

'I have no idea where she is,' Emily said. 'I've looked everywhere and I can't find her.' Finbarr had brought his big hamper with him, in which to carry off the animals to their new home. He set it down on the floor of the shop and to his astonishment, Presto immediately hopped into it, followed by one of the marmalade kittens.

'No, no,' said Keira to Alexander, 'it's Mulvey who's going in the hamper, not you.' She picked up the little ball of fluff and put it in its own basket but when she turned back to the hamper again, the second kitten was already there in its place. Aloysius wriggled and mewed as she lifted him out, and while she was busy with that, Alexander sneaked back in again. All the while Captain Cockle was looping the loop and squawking, making such a racket that Keira and Emily and Finbarr could hardly hear themselves think.

At last Keira and Finbarr managed to get the kittens out of the hamper. 'Now you, Mr Bunny-Rabbit,' Finbarr said sternly. 'Off you go.' He picked up the side of the hamper and tilted it, so that the rabbit would be forced to hop out. But a very strange thing happened – Presto seemed to be stuck to the bottom of the hamper. Finbarr and Emily stared at each other in amazement. 'How is that happening?' Finbarr said. He tilted the basket to an even steeper angle and still Presto sat there and didn't fall out. 'I probably shouldn't do this,' Finbarr muttered, 'but I'm going to try.' He picked the hamper up in both hands and held it upside down…and still Presto didn't fall out! It was as if he was glued to the bottom of the hamper.

'It's like magic!' Emily said. Presto gave an upside-down smile. Finbarr put the hamper back on the floor the right way up and immediately both kittens jumped in again and sat down.

For some moments now Keira had been staring at Noreen in her tank. She was coiled up in a funny heap this morning. There seemed to be more of her than usual. How could that be? She looked at her even more closely and then noticed, peering out from deep in the middle of her coils, two small, bright brown eyes. 'Auntie Emily,' she said, 'I think I've found Bubbles.'

By the time Finbarr had spent twenty minutes trying, and failing, to unwind Noreen from around Bubbles, he was at his wits' end. Presto and the kittens were still in the hamper, Mulvey was still on his high shelf and Captain Cockle was still in the air.

Suddenly Emily burst into tears. 'Oh, my mother was right, I should never have bought a pet shop! I should have listened to what she said and opened a tea room instead. I'm no good with animals, no good at all.'

As soon as she said this, extraordinary things began to happen. Noreen went limp and loose, so that Bubbles almost fell into Finbarr's hands. Presto and the kittens got out of the hamper and scampered back to their rightful places in the shop. Captain Cockle came to rest on his perch and fell silent, while Mulvey scooted down the curtains, walked straight across the floor, got into the hamper and sat down with his paws folded neatly before him. Finbarr put Bubbles in beside the cat and they gazed up at him expectantly.

'Off we go then?' Finbarr said. And he could have sworn that all three creatures nodded back.

In the Castle

Even though he had lived all his life in Gillnacurry, Finbarr had never once had his toes across the threshold of the castle until that morning, when he delivered the animals to their new home. Mrs Fysshe-Pye herself opened the heavy oak door to him.

'Wipe your feet,' she said in greeting, 'and walk this way.'

Holding the hamper tightly and with a glum Captain Cockle perched on his shoulder,

Finbarr followed her down the hall. He did his best not to stand on the trailing shawls and scarves which, he discovered, Henrietta wore even when she was indoors, even on a bright summer day. The hall was long, dark and gloomy, with mouldy old tapestries on the walls and weird-looking sets of antlers hanging above the doorways. There was silence but for the sound of her tinkling silver bracelets. The whole place gave Finbarr the creeps, and he felt so sorry for the poor creatures who were going to have to live there.

Henrietta led the way into by far the biggest room Finbarr had ever seen in his entire life. If he narrowed his eyes and looked carefully, he could just about see to the far end of it. Ever so high above his head there was a vaulted ceiling made of wooden beams. The floor was made of stone, and despite the few shabby rugs that covered it, the cold seeped into Finbarr's feet and up his legs in a strange and unpleasant way. The small fire that crackled in a massive fireplace made the room no warmer. There was a leather armchair before the fire and from the depths of it, came a tiny voice.

'Hello Finbarr. Have you brought us our animals?'

Finbarr realised who it was as Ryan slid out of the immense chair and stood before him on a faded rug.

'May I hold the parrot, please?'

Finbarr took the gaudy bird from his own shoulder and carefully set it on the little boy's outstretched arm. Then he opened the hamper and lifted out the cat and the terrier.

As he did this, something very peculiar happened. The animals appeared to shrink. Mulvey, who was a most impressive-looking creature, suddenly seemed diminished and small. Bubbles, who was a tiny little pooch in the first place, almost disappeared.

'I liked them more when they were in the shop,' Henrietta said, peering down at the two animals. 'They seemed bigger. The cat looks particularly insignificant.'

'That's only because this place is too big, Mummy. Everything looks the wrong size in here.'

'The castle is big, but it's not too big, Ryan. How many times do I have to tell you that? You're a most ungrateful boy. Every single child in this town is envious of you because of where you live.'

Finbarr knew that this wasn't true. He knew of at least one child whom he felt certain would much rather live in a pretty, ivy-covered cottage than in this cold and creepy castle, and he suspected that all the other children in Gillnacurry probably felt the same.

From his pocket he took a folded sheet of paper, and handed it to Henrietta. 'Emily asked me to give you this. It's a list of all their feeding requirements and their daily routines. I'll just nip out to the lorry and get the rest of the stuff.'

Henrietta had insisted on new equipment for the animals, even though Emily had told her they would be quite happy with the things they already had.

As soon as he was out of the castle and standing in the sunshine Finbarr was tempted to jump in his lorry and drive off as fast as he could. But he did as he had said and carried in the new kennel, perch and basket, together with a carton containing a supply of food to start them off.

'That will be all,' said Mrs Fysshe-Pye. 'You can see yourself out.'

It broke Finbarr's heart to see the three creatures looking so forlorn. 'Goodbye my little friends!' he whispered as he stroked Mulvey, whose ears had gone quite flat on his head. 'I know you'll look after each other.' Bubbles whimpered and Captain Cockle shifted uneasily from foot to foot.

'Goodbye, my dears, goodbye. Good luck!'

Henrietta and the Animals

As soon as Finbarr had gone, Henrietta glanced over the sheet of paper that Emily had sent her. 'What nonsense is this? They don't need anything like as much food as she says, I'm quite sure of it. It would do the cat good to go on a diet, it's terribly fat.'

'No he isn't, Mummy.' Ryan had set Captain Cockle on his perch and was now gently cuddling Mulvey, in an attempt to cheer him up. 'He feels quite thin under his fur. I'm sure he needs whatever the pet shop lady says to give him.'

'Mangos!' Henrietta went on, still looking at the sheet of paper and not responding to her son. 'Pineapples! Goodness me, spoilt rotten these animals are. They're going to mend their ways now that they're living with me, just see if they don't. The first thing we must do is give them new names.'

'Why?' Ryan protested. 'They're probably used to the names they already have and don't want to be called something different.'

'Fluff,' cried Henrietta, as if she hadn't heard a word her son said. 'That's what we'll call the cat, Fluff. And as for the dog, now let me see.' She stared down at Bubbles with her great, round eyes for some moments. 'What about Bones? That's a good name for a dog, don't you think?'

'If you say so then I suppose it is.'

'Don't be sulky, Ryan,' his mother said sharply. 'I won't put up with it. That only leaves the parrot. I wonder if it can talk? That woman in the shop was crafty, she never mentioned it. If it can't talk, I should have got ten per cent off, at the very least. Pretty Polly! Pretty Polly! Come along Birdie, are you stupid or just stubborn? Repeat after me. Pretty Polly! Pretty Polly!'

Just at that moment there was a mad outburst of barking at Henrietta's ankles, a sort of loud, *Arf! Arf! Arf!* laced through with a terrible whining sound. 'What is it, you silly dog, what's wrong with you?'

'You stood on her paw, Mummy. You hurt her.'

'I hope you don't blame me for that. She's so tiny, such a ridiculously small dog. She's bound to get under my feet from time to time, a little titch like that. Move out of my way, Bones.'

'It's not her fault. I don't care what you say Mummy, this castle is too big. The animals will be rattling around in it just like we are.'

'Any minute now, I'm going to get very cross indeed. My castle is NOT too big. The dog is too small, the cat is too fat and the parrot is either stupid or sly. They are all going to change from now on. You, Fluff, for a start,' and she picked him up by the scruff of his neck. 'You are going to have to work for your keep. You will catch mice for me or I'll want to know the reason why. That pet shop woman may have let you do what you want and spoiled you all rotten, but believe you me, those days are gone!'

Mulvey and the Mouse

In the following days, Ryan did his best to look after Mulvey, Bubbles and Captain Cockle but his mother was always interfering and scolding. How the animals hated their new home! It was draughty and uncomfortable and much too big.

Late one evening, not long after his arrival, Mulvey had had his dinner, a miserable meal, and was sitting in front of the drawing room fire trying to get warm, when suddenly

Henrietta gave a loud shriek.

'EEEK! A MOUSE! A MOUSE!'

Mulvey looked around. Standing over by the window was a tiny wee creature, so small in the great room that the cat had to narrow its eyes and peer hard to see it properly.

'She's absolutely right,' he thought. 'It is a mouse.'

Although it was brown rather than white it reminded him of his four little friends back in the shop. With a sigh, he turned away and was gazing into the fire again when ker-thunk! Something hit him on the side of the head. Henrietta had actually thrown a shoe at him!

'What are you waiting for, Fluff, you stupid cat? Catch it! Kill it!' And she screamed again.

With that, the mouse took off. It zipped across the rug and out through the door of the drawing room; and Mulvey, hardly knowing what he was doing, ran after it. The mouse raced down the long, long hall, past the faded tapestries and the antlers. It shot up the great stone stairs of the castle with Mulvey still chasing it and panting hard with the effort to keep up, trying desperately not to let it get away. On they ran, past suits of armour and four-poster beds until Mulvey thought his lungs would burst. Like most cats, he was rather lazy and what he had always liked best was loafing around in his basket, cracking jokes and making the other animals in the shop laugh. He did NOT like running. Oh, where was this wretched mouse going and would it ever get there?

They came to more steps, a narrow wooden staircase this time, down which the mouse shot with the cat after it. Mulvey arrived at the bottom just in time to see the mouse vanish behind a half-open door, which the cat also entered. To his relief he found himself at a dead end, in a relatively small room. He stopped running and closed his eyes, tried hard to get his breath back.

'Oh please Fluff, please! Don't kill me and

eat me!' Mulvey opened his eyes again and saw that the mouse was kneeling before him, with an anguished look on its face. 'Stand up. And don't call me Fluff.' This clearly astonished the mouse. 'That's what SHE calls me, but it isn't my name. Fluff is what people find under the bed if they're not too fussy about housework. It is not, repeat *not*, a suitable name for a cat like me. I'm Mulvey. And do stand up, you're beginning to annoy me, kneeling there. Who are you, anyway?'

'I'm – I'm Fergal,' said the mouse, as it cautiously got to its feet.

'Pleased to meet you.' The mouse trembled and almost fainted. 'Not "eat", MEET! I said MEET! Look, let's get this clear – I don't like mice.' Immediately, Mulvey realised that this sounded a bit rude. 'I mean, I like them as friends, they can be great company, but I have no interest whatsoever in them as food. Few cats do.'

'But you chase mice. You chased me.'

'So what? Dogs chase cars, but they don't eat them, do they?'

'I suppose not,' said Fergal. He rubbed his nose with his paw and thought about this.

'Anyway, why would I eat you when here we are, surrounded by loads and loads of lovely grub?' And Mulvey gave a slow grin. To his great delight he had just realised that the room into which he had chased the mouse was the larder of the castle. He sprang up onto the nearest shelf. 'Kippers. Yum! I don't know when I last had a kipper. What about you, Fergal? What would you like? Fruit cake? Cream crackers? An apple, perhaps?'

'I wouldn't mind a few peanuts, if you'd be so kind as to push them off the shelf for me. They're over there by the fruit bowl.'

The cat narrowed its eyes and looked down at the mouse with a sly smile. 'You know your way about in here, don't you? Maybe you've been here before?'

Fergal in his turn gave a crafty smile.

'Perhaps I have,' he said.

And the cat and the mouse burst out laughing together.

What a feast they had! Kippers and peanuts were only the start of it. Just as they were beginning to feel that neither of them could eat another bite, there was a sharp rap on the door.

'Fluff! What are you doing? Have you caught that mouse yet? I know you're both in there.'

'Hmm, I'd almost forgotten about her. Now, how do we deal with this? Here's a suggestion,' said Mulvey, and he hopped down from the shelf again. 'We'll pretend I've caught you. You get into my mouth – don't worry, I'll be careful not to hurt you – and I'll carry you out of here, set you at her feet. She'll scream a bit and then she'll put you in the bin, or more likely, get Ryan to do it. All you have to do is stay as still as you can during all of this, then wait in the bin until night-time when everyone's asleep. Then you climb out of the bin and go home. That sounds like a pretty good plan to me. What do you think?'

'I suppose it would work,' said the mouse, faintly.

'Right, let's get weaving. In you hop,' and the cat opened its mouth wide.

For some moments Fergal stood staring into Mulvey's maw, so pink and moist, with its neat rows of savage-looking teeth. Much as he liked the cat, to climb into a mouth like that was a terrifying idea to him. It went against everything he had ever been taught as a mouse. It was completely unnatural to him. He did his very best to be brave, but at last he said in a shaky voice, 'Mulvey, I'm sorry. I'm so, so sorry but I just can't do this.'

The cat closed its mouth and looked down. He saw how upset the mouse was. 'Don't worry, it was just an idea. I'm sure we can think of something else.'

'Couldn't you simply chase me back to where I live? I'm sure we could make it look convincing. Just give me ten seconds of a head start.'

They talked it over and that was what they decided to do.

'Only this time Fergal, go straight home, eh? No running about upstairs.'

'I promise, Mulvey.'

'Under starter's orders!' The mouse crouched down, took up position like a sprinter. 'On your marks...

...get ready...

...get set...

...GO!

GO FERGAL GO!'

The mouse zoomed out of the larder. Henrietta screeched. The cat started its countdown. 'Ten, nine, eight...' Now Mulvey was preparing to run. After his big meal, it was the last thing he wanted to do, but there was no alternative. '...Three, two, one – off!' He raced out as fast as he could, and was just in time to see Fergal turn the corner at the bottom of the corridor.

Gosh, this was hard work. He might not have had that last piece of pork pie if he had known this was going to happen.

'Catch it, Fluff! Kill it!'

'Fat chance, even if I wanted to,' Mulvey thought, as he began the long, long trek down the hall. Where do mice get their energy from, he wondered. Fergal looked as fresh and fit as when he had first started running – looked as if he could keep going for hours. Puffing and panting, gasping for breath, Mulvey at last came to the drawing room, with Henrietta at his heels. He was just in time to see Fergal put on a final spurt, and make it across the rug to his mouse hole.

'Goodbye, Mulvey! Thanks for everything!'

'Cheers, Fergal! Good luck!'

'You stupid cat! You're useless. Useless!'

Ker-thunk! And Henrietta threw her other shoe at him.

Mulvey has a Good Idea

Deep in the castle in the middle of the night, Mulvey lay awake in his basket wondering what time it was. He missed hearing the familiar sound of the angels chiming the hours, for the castle was far from the pet shop and the church. All he could hear in his new home was the sound of the great golden fish on the wind-vane, creaking as it turned, a noise the cat found quite sinister. He rolled over and tried to get comfortable, for he still wasn't used to his new basket, with its stiff, prickly blanket. How he longed for his familiar old nest back in the shop, with its wicker broken in places, and his beloved tartan rug! Tears welled up in his huge sapphire eyes and he struggled to blink them away.

Yesterday had been a particularly horrible day. Bubbles, who was always getting lost, had been missing for longer than ever before. Ryan, the sweet child, had searched all over the castle and eventually found the little dog down the back of a sofa, together with an old biro and a handful of loose change. Mulvey himself had been given no dinner because he had torn Henrietta's tights to shreds, deliberately, it has to be said. He simply lost his temper after hearing her nag Captain Cockle for over an hour about refusing to talk. As she walked past Mulvey he lashed out with his claws, and to his satisfaction managed to scratch her shins as well as rip her tights. Any animal, if badly treated, is likely to turn nasty, and who can blame it? Ryan got no dinner either, because Henrietta caught him trying to sneak a few cat treats to Mulvey when her back was turned. The cat rolled over again in the basket and his tummy rumbled loudly.

They had been in the castle for just over a week now but it seemed more like several months. Ah, his dear old friends from the past! In recent days he had tried not to think about them because it made him feel so sad and lonely, but now he closed his eyes and remembered them all with such fondness. He thought of plump little Betty, running on her wheel. Then there were Alexander and Aloysius the marmalade kittens. What a fine pair they would be when they grew up, a credit to the cat kingdom. He thought about Presto and how his nose used to twitch. Mulvey remembered Noreen and how they used to tease her, how they all used to chorus, 'Oh she's lovely and warm, she feels just like a handbag!'

He thought about Presto again.

Then he thought about the white mice, that squirming tangle of paws and whiskers and tails and snouts, Milly and Willy and Tilly and Billy.

He thought about Presto again.

The tropical fish that—

He thought about Presto.

He thought about Presto.

He thought about Presto.

Suddenly, the cat opened wide his round blue eyes and stared into the darkness. He had just had a very good idea.

Deep in the castle, in the middle of the night, a slow grin crept across Mulvey's face.

Escape!

There was no time to lose. Mulvey jumped out of his basket and set off to look for Bubbles and Captain Cockle. The parrot slept on his perch in the drawing-room; he would go there first.

How tiny the cat looked as he moved through the vast castle! He padded down the long, long hall carpet until he came to the drawing room door which, like all the doors, was made of solid, heavy oak. It was open but only by the tiniest crack. The gap was much too narrow for Mulvey to slip through and so he pushed the door with his paw. Well, that is, he tried to push but it might as well have been a stone wall for all the difference it made. He sat up on his back legs and tried again, this time using both of his front paws and pushing as hard as he could, but still the door wouldn't budge. Mulvey then put his shoulder to it but it was no use, and he fell back panting for breath. Oh this was dreadful! He simply had to get into the room.

Angry now, he drew back and crouched down. Mulvey pulled all his energy into the core of himself, concentrating it as he made himself as small as he could possibly be, rocking almost imperceptibly from side to side, as if he were stalking a bird or a mouse.

And then he sprang.

The cat hit the door at about six foot off the ground and it flew open. There was an almighty crash and then wild, mad squawking.

Mulvey, unable to stop himself, tumbled into the room and somersaulted across the faded rug until he came to a halt by banging into a sideboard. Sitting up, he rubbed the bump on the top of his head and looking around, realised what had happened. When he'd forced the door open he'd literally knocked Captain Cockle off his perch, which was now lying on the floor. The parrot, meanwhile, was still flying around in circles, squawking and swooping like a demented thing.

'Shut your beak! It's me, Mulvey. Stop that racket or you'll wake Henrietta.'

Astonished, the parrot settled on top of the fireplace and fell silent. They listened for a few moments for footsteps but none came.

'What are you doing here?' Captain Cockle eventually dared to ask. 'What's happening?'

'I've come to take you home,' the cat said smoothly. 'Let's go and find Bubbles.'

At Mulvey's suggestion, the parrot sat on the cat's back and they set off for the kennel where the terrier slept. Although he didn't say so, Mulvey didn't quite trust the parrot not to fly into something and make a noise again (quite forgetting that it was he, Mulvey, who had brought about all the chaos in the drawing room). For his part, Captain Cockle had never travelled by cat before and was surprised to find how much he enjoyed it. It was swift and smooth; and it was something of a novelty for him to be moving along at speed so close to the ground.

'I could get used to this, Mulvey,'

'In your dreams, mate.'

Bubbles' kennel was located near the kitchen door, and they smelt it long before they saw it. Like the cat's basket and the perch, it had been brand new a week ago and still reeked of fresh paint.

'Psst! Bubbles! It's us. Are you asleep?'

A bright and familiar little face popped out of the kennel. 'With this stink? No way. But what's happening? Why are you here?'

'We're going home!' cried Captain Cockle. 'Mulvey's taking us back to the pet shop.'

'What?! How on earth are you going to do that?'

'By magic,' said the cat. The other two creatures stared at him in amazement. 'Don't you remember the first night Presto came to the shop and I teased him; I told him he didn't know how magic was done?'

'And then he told you – he whispered in your ear?'

The cat nodded. 'Precisely. And I think I remember enough from what he said to be able to get us home again.'

'You think you remember?' said Bubbles. 'You *think*?'

'I'm pretty sure, yes, and it's worth a shot anyway.' Captain Cockle and Bubbles looked at each other.

'What d'you reckon?' said the parrot.

'It's a big risk, isn't it?' said Bubbles.

'Yes, it is. And what if it all goes wrong?

What if we end up in the middle of a big city or at the North Pole, or in Doris Crump's house? From what Presto said she might be even worse than Henrietta. What then, Mulvey? Have you thought about that?'

'It all sounds very dangerous to me, I must say, very dangerous indeed.'

For a moment the cat did not speak and then it said in a low calm voice, 'There is not the slightest doubt in my mind that if I were here with Alexander and Aloysius instead of with you pair that they would agree with my plan immediately. And shall I tell you why? Because they are fearless. Because they are full of bravery and courage. Because even though they look like two tiny little specks of orange fluff and are cute enough to have their photograph on a calendar, they have hearts like lions. And why is this? Let me tell you why. It is, my dear friends, because THEY ARE CATS!'

During this short speech, Bubbles and Captain Cockle had looked increasingly uncomfortable.

'Now hold on a minute, Mulvey. We didn't say we wouldn't do it and we didn't say we were afraid. We're just aware of the risks. We're only being sensible, aren't we, Bubbles?'

'Absolutely. Being brave is one thing, being reckless is something else entirely. The thing is this—'

But before Bubbles could finish, Mulvey had silenced him with a raised paw. 'Are you coming with me or not?'

Bubbles and Captain Cockle stared at each other again, then Bubbles looked down at her paws. The parrot shifted uneasily from claw to claw and then mumbled something under its breath, something like 'Min.'

'I'm sorry, could you repeat that please?' said the cat sharply. 'I didn't quite catch it.

'I said, I'm in.'

'Good. Bubbles?'

The terrier looked up and took a deep breath. 'I'm in too.'

'Excellent,' said Mulvey and he grinned. It was his old familiar foxy grin, full of mischief and good humour and it made the others smile too. Like all cats, Mulvey was not one to bear a grudge.

'What do we have to do?'

'It's quite simple,' said Mulvey. 'We all have to be touching when I say the magic words and we all have to keep our eyes closed. What I suggest is that you, Bubbles, climb up on to my back and that Captain Cockle then perches on top of you.'

It was easier said than done. Bubbles' paws kept slipping against Mulvey's fur and she found it terribly hard to keep her balance. 'Oooh, it's all wobbly! I don't like it!'

'Do your best, it's only for a moment. Now you, Captain Cockle, as gently and as carefully as you can, fly down and land on Bubbles' back.'

Try as they might, it didn't work. As soon as the parrot landed on the dog she fell off the cat and all three collapsed in a great heap of feathers and fur.

'Plan B,' said Mulvey, gingerly pushing the parrot off his head. 'We try again only this time I go in the middle.'

This worked much better. Bubbles stood four square on the floor and Mulvey, who had quite an extraordinary sense of balance, placed all four of his paws in the middle of the dog's back, pressed into the tiniest space imaginable. He was as steady as a rock, and when the parrot joined them there was no wobbling this time.

'Great stuff! Just think, in a split second from now we'll be back in the shop with Noreen and all the gang. What a surprise they're going to get! Now then, here we go. Eyes tightly closed please and keep them closed until we arrive. One, two three...'

All three animals squeezed their eyes closed as tight as tight could be, and Mulvey started to mutter under his breath, then shouted aloud: 'ABRACADABRA!'

Whoosh! They took off like a firework. Up and up they went, so hard and fast that Mulvey's ears were pressed flat against his head. He wondered if they would ever recover. Would they ever again pop up into the triumphant points of chocolate-coloured fur of which he was secretly so proud?

'Arrgh! This is horrible! I want my Mammy!' Bubbles shrieked.

'We're going to crash through the roof!' cried Captain Cockle. 'I'll get my head smashed in!'

'Don't be daft. We've long since left the castle.'

'But how can that be?'

'It's magic!' the cat shouted.

They were still, amazingly, as they were when they had set out, with the parrot balanced on the cat and the cat standing on the dog. Just when they thought they wouldn't be able to endure the speed and the pressure for a moment longer, suddenly they came to an abrupt halt.

If they had been like a rocket going up, they were like a rocket coming down too. They drifted apart from each other and, like soft wisps of coloured flame, they began to fall slowly through the air, gently, gently.

'Are you both still there?' Mulvey cried.

'Yes! Yes!'

'Don't open your eyes. Keep them tightly shut, whatever you do.'

This falling experience was quite pleasant – certainly it was more agreeable than the swift ascent. Mulvey was relieved to feel his ears spring back to normal. Suddenly a horrible thought struck him. They had gone straight up and seemed to be coming straight down. What if they ended up back where they'd started, in Henrietta's castle? What if, in the moment of their departure, they had actually blown a hole through the roof? They were bound to get the blame, even if she had no idea how they had done it.

Down and down they floated, and just when they were beginning to wonder if they would ever arrive anywhere or if perhaps this descent would go on forever, with the softest *bump* imaginable they came to earth.

'Are you there, Captain Cockle?'

'Yes I am.'

'Me too,' said Bubbles. 'Can we open our eyes now, Mulvey?'

'I think so. On the count of three. One, two, three!'

With thumping hearts and knees trembling in fright, the three friends slowly opened their eyes and looked around.

Lost in the Night

They weren't in the castle any longer, but they weren't in the pet shop either. 'Where are we?' cried Captain Cockle.

'I haven't a clue,' Mulvey admitted. There was grass under his paws and a gentle breeze blowing, so he knew that they were out in the open air, but it was a coal-black night and even the cat could see nothing.

'What if we're hundreds and hundreds of miles from home? What if we're in another country? We'll never get back to Gillnacurry, we'll never see Emily and Keira again, nor Noreen and Betty and all the others. Oh this is terrible,' cried Captain Cockle. 'You should never have listened to that rabbit, Mulvey, and we shouldn't have listened to you.'

'At least we're away from Henrietta,' the cat said. 'And at least I did something. We could have been stuck there for years and years.'

Just with that, a huge full moon appeared, as the dark cloud that had been covering it slowly drifted away. The three friends found themselves bathed in a strange, silvery light that was pale, but surprisingly strong, so that they could see each other clearly. They could also see some trees and that they were standing on the top of a hill so that they seemed to be level with the full moon. Mulvey felt that if he were to reach out with his paw, he would be able to touch it. Beside them there was an odd dark object, the size of a small child, and as they walked over to take a closer look, it stood out black against the moon, with the exception of a small perfect circle in the middle of it, which was filled with silvery light.

'I know where we are!' Bubbles shouted. 'It's the holey stone! We ARE still in Gillnacurry! Why, I used to come here every morning with Keira.' She started to bark in sheer delight, and bounced up and down. Mulvey scampered around like a mad kitten instead of the stately old cat he really was, while Captain Cockle flew in great loops in the air above them, cackling with laughter, before perching on the very top of the holey stone itself.

'That's wonderful, Bubbles!' said Mulvey. 'After you!'

'What do you mean, after me?'

'Well if you come here every morning you must know the way back to the shop, so Captain Cockle and I will follow you. Let's go, it's getting cold standing out here.'

Bubbles was silent for a moment. 'I think it's

quite nice here,' she said at last, 'We could wait a while longer. I mean now we know where we are, what's the rush to get home?'

Now it was Mulvey who fell silent and then after a long, sinister pause he said, 'You don't know the way, do you? You came here every single day and you don't know the way home.' Bubbles said nothing, and Mulvey knew he was right. 'You paid no attention to where you were,' the cat went on, as its tail began to twitch. 'You let Keira do all the work and you were just at the end of the lead, not noticing anything except lamp-posts and trees and other dogs. And a fat lot of use that is to us now!'

'You got us into this mess in the first place,' Bubbles said, and Mulvey's eyes grew cold and hard.

'I beg your pardon? Are you blaming ME for this? Would you like to go back to the castle, to that horrible woman? Because with the magic Presto taught me I could send you back on your own, and Captain Cockle and I will stay here. Is that what you want? Would you like that?'

'Bet you couldn't,' said Bubbles. 'You're rubbish at magic,' but the cat could see that she was worried.

Mulvey smiled. 'You're right,' he said. 'I'm not an expert. You might not end up in the castle. You might end up thousands and thousands of miles away. We might never see you again. But I can always try. ABRACAD—'

'NO! NO!' screamed Bubbles. 'Please don't, Mulvey. I'm sorry I don't know the way home but I don't want to go back to Henrietta and I don't want to get lost, to be with people who don't know who I am. Please don't put a spell on me.'

Mulvey shook his head and clicked his tongue. 'Dogs. I ask you!' he said. 'Supposed to be man's best friend. Supposed to be INTELLIGENT. All that running after sticks in the park doesn't fool us for a moment. All cats know that dogs are as thick as planks.'

Bubbles couldn't let this pass and was just about to argue with Mulvey when Captain Cockle suddenly said, 'Shush! Somebody spoke! Didn't you hear it? Somebody said, "Who are you?"'

'I didn't hear anything,' said Bubbles.

''Course you didn't, bone-head,' said Mulvey. 'Dum-dum dogs don't listen, just like they don't pay any attention to where they're going on their morning walk. But I heard it. And you're wrong,' he added to the parrot. 'It didn't say, "Who are you?", it was more like, "Hoo-witt-hoo-woo!"'

'It didn't, Mulvey,' Captain Cockle insisted, but before a new argument could start a small clear voice from just above their heads said, 'You're both right. Or maybe you're both wrong. Anyway, what I said was, "Hoo-witt-hoo-woo! Who are you?"'

The three animals gasped in astonishment. Who could it possibly be?

A Little Helper

Sitting on a branch of a tree high above them was something that looked like a little heap of soft, creamy-coloured feathers, from which peered two eyes. They were round, like Mulvey's, and the creature's face was quite flat, like Mulvey's; it was even something similar in colour to Mulvey, and yet in spite of all this they did not look remotely like each other. For one thing, this creature's eyes were not blue like the cat's, but yellow as topaz.

It had an odd little beak and claws for feet. The baby owl – for that is what it was – was staring hard at Captain Cockle, who was still perched on top of the holey stone.

'I was talking to you,' said the little bird. 'Look at you! Oh just look at you! You're beautiful, you are. Who are you? Your feathers are amazing colours. How did they get to be like that? Did you paint them?'

''Course not,' said Captain Cockle proudly. 'I was born like this.'

'Never!' gasped the baby owl. 'Where are you from?'

'Brazil, actually.'

Mulvey snorted with laughter when he heard this. 'Brazil, your granny! You're from Gillnacurry, just like the rest of us.'

'No I'm not. I'm an Amazonian Rainforest Parrot and they come from Brazil. Everybody knows that.'

'Well I'm a Persian cat but I don't go around pretending to be from Persia. If you're from

Brazil, say something to us in Portuguese.'

'Portuguese? Why?' asked the parrot.

'That's the language you Brazilians speak,' said Mulvey. 'Didn't you know that?'

''Course I did. But I've sort of forgotten all my Portuguese now. It's a long time since I was there, I haven't spoken it for years,' said Captain Cockle, who was looking very embarrassed.

By now the baby owl was staring hard at Mulvey. 'You look really strange. You're a cat, aren't you?'

'No, I'm a kangaroo,' said Mulvey sarcastically. 'Of course I'm a cat, you nit-wit.'

'You look really strange,' the baby owl said again. 'I've seen lots of cats in Gillnacurry and none of them are like you. You're really woolly and you've got no nose.'

'Better that than to have NO NECK!' shouted the cat, glaring up at the branch. 'Better to have woolly fur than to look like some kind of EXPLODED PILLOW, I'd have thought.'

'Please little bird,' said Bubbles softly, 'can you help us? We're lost. Let me tell you our story.' And so while the cat simmered with rage beside her, the dog explained to the baby owl everything that had happened. It took quite a while, for there were so many things the owl didn't know about, like pet shops and magic shows and magicians' rabbits. She had just started to explain what salt and vinegar crisps were when Mulvey interrupted.

'Oh get to the point, Bubbles, for goodness sake. Look here, you,' he went on, turning his face up to where the baby owl was sitting. 'You know the church with the clock tower in the middle of town? The one with the angels on it?'

''Course I do. Everybody knows it.'

'Bet you couldn't take us there.'

'I could, too,' said the baby owl.

'No you couldn't,' the cat insisted. 'You're too little. You'd get lost.'

'I would not!'

'Would!'

'Wouldn't!'

'Would!'

'Wouldn't!'

'All right then,' said the cat, 'prove it.'

'I'll take you there immediately,' said the baby owl in a huffy voice. 'The Amazonian Rainforest Parrot and I will fly on ahead of you and the dog a little bit, and wait until you catch up. Then we'll fly on again and you can follow us. All right?'

'We'll give it a try,' Mulvey said and he shrugged indifferently, but as soon as he knew that the baby bird wasn't looking, the cat grinned at Bubbles and gave her a broad wink. The dog was beginning to have to admit, if only to herself, that cats actually were very smart indeed.

And so the little band set off. Captain Cockle and the baby owl flew down the hill and sat on a bush chatting until such time as the cat and dog caught up with them. 'So what was it like being on a pirate ship, then?' the baby owl was saying breathlessly as the other two arrived.

'Just amazing. I'll tell you all about it when we stop again,' said Captain Cockle. 'How's it going down there?'

'Fine, fine,' panted Mulvey, who was finding it hard-going but who wasn't prepared to admit it.

'See you soon!' cried the parrot, as he and the baby owl soared effortlessly into the night sky. Mulvey and Bubbles watched them fly through the moonlit air, saw them settle in the far distance on a low wall and then began to plod wearily towards them.

When they finally got to where the two birds were waiting for them, Captain Cockle was explaining to the baby owl what mermaids were. 'They're a bit vain, but they can be quite nice when you get to know them. Ah, there you are! Come along! Follow us!' And they were off again before Mulvey and Bubbles had time to catch their breath.

The two angels in their coloured sashes, one

red and one blue, had just rung four dings on their bell for IV in the morning, and were about to doze off for the next fifty-nine minutes when something quite remarkable happened. First, two extraordinary birds swooped right past their noses. One was a small, creamy-coloured plump bird, with the softest feathers imaginable. The other was so brightly coloured it was hard to believe that it was real, for it was red and green and yellow and blue. The two birds flew once around the square and came to rest upon the windowsill of Emily's pet shop. As the angels craned their necks to stare down at them, they saw two other creatures enter the square: an exhausted looking terrier and a rather bedraggled cat.

'You see! I did know the way after all!' cried the baby owl, delighted with itself, as Mulvey and Bubbles staggered up to the door of the shop.

'Bully for you,' grumbled the cat. 'Thanks, and all that. You'd better head back; your mum will be beginning to wonder where you've got to, a little thing like you out at night.'

'This has been the most exciting thing that has ever happened to me in my whole life,' the small bird sighed, gazing with adoration at Captain Cockle. 'Do you think I could ask you a tiny little favour?'

'Anything you like,' said the parrot, beaming, but the smile slipped from his face when the baby owl said, 'Do you think I could have a feather as a souvenir? Because otherwise, tomorrow this is all just going to seem like a wonderful dream.'

'Um, well now, that might be a little difficult, much as I would like to because you see the thing is... YEOW!' And Captain Cockle leapt off the windowsill clutching his bum. 'Oh, you shouldn't have done that, Mulvey. That hurt!'

'Here you are, Diddums,' the cat said, holding out a long, vivid green tail feather to the baby owl. 'Now beat it. Sorry about that,

Captain, but the night's not over yet and I'm not staying here until morning. We still have things to do.'

As the owl flew away Mulvey hopped up onto the windowsill and opened his mouth as wide as he could.

'MEEEEEAAAAAARRRRGGGGHHHHHHWW WWWOOOOO!'

A window flew up on the far side of the square, and someone threw out an old boot. 'Hi you! Shut your gob, you miserable cat,' a man's voice shouted. 'Some of us are trying to sleep.'

'Oh don't be so rude! I wasn't talking to you anyway, whoever you are,' Mulvey hissed irritably, glancing over his shoulder. Then he turned back and let fly again.

'WWWWWOOOOOMMMMMAAAAAAGOO OOOOOAAAAH!'

All of a sudden, one of the white mice popped up on the other side of the window, knees knocking in fright.

'Get the rabbit,' Mulvey mouthed silently through the glass. 'GET THE RABBIT!'

The mouse vanished, and moments later Presto appeared. He was clearly astonished to see the three friends, but he knew exactly what to do, for he closed his eyes, furrowed his brow, and his nose twitched faster than ever. He muttered something under his breath and then all of a sudden...*BANG!*

Mulvey, Bubbles and Captain Cockle were back in Emily's pet shop.

Home Again

As dawn broke over the little town, the three friends sat up telling all the other animals in the shop about their adventures in the castle and how they had managed to escape from Henrietta. The rabbit was impressed that from the brief chat he had had with Mulvey on that first night, the cat had been able to remember enough magic to set them free, even if they had ended up lost on the hillside.

'What happened to your tail?' Noreen asked

Captain Cockle. 'Did that nasty woman snaffle one of your feathers to put in her best hat?'

Mulvey looked very embarrassed. He was surprised and grateful when the parrot said, 'No, I think it got caught on a bush or just fell out somewhere.' Mulvey felt guilty for having been so grumpy during the night and above all he felt bad about having pulled out the feather.

'Thanks for not telling on me,' he whispered to Captain Cockle as soon as he had the chance.

'Don't mention it,' the parrot whispered back. He felt foolish now to think of all the tall tales he had made up to impress the baby owl and was glad that Mulvey and Bubbles didn't tell the other animals about how boastful he had been.

'But if you were at the holey stone, why did you need help to get home?' asked Betty. 'Didn't you know the way, Bubbles? Didn't Keira used to take you there for a walk every day?'

'Typical hamster!' Bubbles thought. 'They always ask exactly the question you don't want them to ask!' but before she could defend herself Mulvey spoke.

'It was the middle of the night, Betty, and it was pitch-black,' he said.

'But there was a moon!' the hamster insisted.

'You had to be there,' Captain Cockle said. 'It was...confusing, wasn't it?' and Bubbles and Mulvey both nodded. 'Getting the baby owl to help us was a good idea.'

This seemed to satisfy Betty, who asked no more questions. The dog, the cat and the parrot winked at each other, their friendship stronger than ever after all they had been through together.

'Sky's gone pink,' Bubbles said, staring out of the window. 'Gosh, I'm tired.'

'Me too. And hungry,' Mulvey added. 'A whole can of meat chunks in gravy and a pint of milk; that's what I want. Then I'm off to my basket for the rest of the day.' He had missed his old basket more than he had cared to admit and was afraid that Emily might have got rid of it while he was away. But there it was in its usual place, with his beloved tartan rug. It was a bit smelly but Mulvey didn't mind, because it was his rug, and also his smell. To have a good feed and then climb into the basket, wrap himself up and sleep for the rest of the day would be bliss.

Time seemed to crawl past. They heard the clink of bottles as the milkman made his delivery. Later, the flap of the letter-box shot up and a handful of letters fell through onto the doormat, but still they waited for Emily and Keira. At long last Bubbles, who stayed by the window keeping watch, saw the big hand of the clock in the tower move to XII and the little hand settle on IX. The angels dinged their bells nine times and then there was the sound of bike wheels whizzing into the square.

'They're here! They're here!' the little dog cried aloud.

128

A Big Surprise for Emily

'Good morning, my de— good gobstoppers!'
Emily exclaimed when she walked into the
shop. She stood there with her mouth hanging
open, looking every bit as dippy as Finbarr;
something the animals had never seen before.

There was Captain Cockle, back on his perch,
there were Mulvey and Bubbles, standing
beside their empty bowls and staring at her
expectantly. She knew immediately what to do.
They were the first three animals in the shop to

be fed that morning. The parrot ate a whole pineapple, and Bubbles scoffed an entire tin of dog food. Hungriest of all was Mulvey, who almost knocked the milk bottle out of Keira's hand as she filled his saucer, who cried and cried again for more food and who eventually waddled off to his basket, curled himself up in a ball and started to snore like a tractor.

'I could understand it if they had just run away,' Emily kept saying to Keira. 'If I had found them sitting on the step this morning, I'd have been surprised, but this just beggars belief. How on earth did they get back into the shop?'

'They didn't come down the chimney,' Keira said, 'because there is no chimney. And they couldn't possibly have climbed through the letterbox.'

'Noreen might be able to manage that, but never Mulvey!' Emily said, and she giggled to think of Mulvey trying to squeeze his great woolly body through the letterbox. She was actually in a very good mood, because however it had happened, she was delighted to have the animals back in the shop. 'I'm sorry I ever sold them to that woman, but they're back here now for keeps.'

Just at that, *clang!* the door of the shop opened and Finbarr came in. 'Hello Keira. Hello Emily, how are you today?' and he gave her a big soppy smile.

'Never better,' she said, beaming. 'Finbarr, you forgot to put your shoes on this morning. You're still wearing your bedroom slippers.'

'Am I? Am I really? Ooh, thanks for telling me, Emily! Parrot's nice. Looks like the one you sold to that woman in the castle.'

'It is the one I sold to that woman in the castle. It's Captain Cockle himself. And Mulvey's back too, and Bubbles.' She was explaining how she had found them that morning and asking him how he thought they had got there when *clang!* the door of the shop opened again.

It was Henrietta.

Trailing her scarves and tinkling her silver bracelets, she had the unfortunate Ryan in tow. 'Good morning,' she said coldly. As soon as she spoke, something quite extraordinary happened. All three animals, who had been snoozing, woke up with a start. Mulvey shot to the top of the curtains, where he sat scowling, the very tip of his tail twitching slowly back and forth. Captain Cockle flew up to join him and Bubbles hopped into Noreen's tank, where she knew Henrietta would never dare to approach her.

'What strange beasts!' she said. 'They look just like the ones you sold me, and they were all trouble-makers too.'

'They are our pets, Mummy,' Ryan said in a sulky voice. 'They ran away from home and came back here, just like I thought they might. They knew you didn't like them. But I did. They were good company. I still think the kittens are nice and the rabbit too.'

'They were useless!' Henrietta said, glaring up at Mulvey, whom she had particularly disliked. 'They were far too small for a castle the size of mine. Don't you have any big pets?'

'Not really,' Emily said.

'What sort of a pet shop is this anyway!' Henrietta said rudely.

'Now you listen to me, Mrs Apple-Pie,' said Finbarr.

'Fysshe!' snapped Henrietta. 'Not "Apple". Fysshe. Fysshe-Pye. Two y's, two e's, two s's and a hyphen. Goodness me, man, how many times do I have to tell you?'

'Sorry, I'm sure,' said Finbarr, who didn't sound a bit sorry. 'Big pets you want, big pets you shall have. Come back at the same time tomorrow morning. Leave it to me, Emily,' he added.

'Leave it to me!'

A Big Surprise for Henrietta

'Finbarr,' Emily said, 'it's a sheep.'

Finbarr nodded happily. 'Right first time,' he said. 'And the other one's a goat. Just the job for Missus Wossername, don't you think? I mean, they're big aren't they? Much bigger than a cat or a terrier.'

Keira and Emily gazed at the sheep and the goat who were both standing there in the middle of the shop floor. They both agreed with Finbarr that the animals were big.

'Where did you get them?' asked Emily.

'From my brother Davy,' Finbarr said. 'He's a farmer.'

Keira patted the sheep on the head and it gave a soft 'baa'. 'I think it's nice,' she said, 'but I don't know if Mrs Fysshe-Pye will like it.'

'We'll soon know,' said Emily glancing at the window, 'because here she comes.'

Clang! The door flew open and in came Henrietta and Ryan.

'Hello Missus!' said Finbarr. 'These are for you.'

Henrietta's eyes grew large with amazement. 'It's a sheep,' she said. 'A sheep and a goat.'

Finbarr nodded and smiled.

'And do you really think, you foolish man, do you really think for a single minute that I would have those horrible animals in my castle?'

'You wanted big animals,' Keira pointed out.

'But they're horribly smelly. I can hardly breathe.'

This, sadly, was true.

'The goat pongs a bit,' Finbarr admitted 'but the sheep's not too bad. I thought you'd really like them. Oh well, no harm done. There's such a demand for animals like this that there's a waiting list. We put you at the top as a special favour, but if you don't want them there's dozens of other people who'll be only too glad to buy them. They're all the rage in Hollywood now, you know. All the film stars are crazy for sheep and goats.'

'Are they?' said Henrietta who was suddenly interested. 'Are they really?'

'It's incredible. Last year the fashion was for pigs, now it's sheep and goats.'

This seemed to ring a bell with Henrietta. 'Hmmm,' she said. 'Now that you mention it, I do remember the pig thing. But wasn't that baby pigs? Small little ones with pot-bellies?'

'Could have been, but this time round, it's sheep and goats and the bigger the better.'

During all of this, Keira had been doing her

best not to laugh out loud. Mulvey seemed to be having the same problem. She glanced over at his basket and saw that he had stuffed the corner of his tartan rug into his mouth and was completely cross-eyed from trying to hold in his giggles. There were waves of snurgles and gulps as all the animals tried not to give the game away. Keira looked at Ryan and to her surprise he grinned broadly at her and winked. Clearly he could see that Finbarr was telling his mother a total load of codswallop, but he didn't seem to mind at all.

'Hmmn,' Henrietta said again. 'If they're all the rage then I simply have to have them. But if I wait and see, I might have to wait for a long time?'

'Could be months,' Finbarr said. 'Could be years even, before a chance like this comes your way again.'

'What do you think, Ryan?'

'I think they're brilliant, Mummy. What are you waiting for?'

Henrietta took out her cheque book and pen. 'Deliver them tomorrow,' she said to Finbarr, with no sign of a 'please' or a 'thank you'.

She swept out of the shop and Emily, Keira and Finbarr collapsed in laughter. Only Keira noticed that all the animals were laughing too.

Two New Friends

'So what are your names then?' said Bubbles.

It was past midnight, and all the animals in the shop crowded around the area, blocked off with bales of hay, which Finbarr had marked out as a temporary pen for the new arrivals.

'I'm Nora,' said the sheep, 'and this is Nobby.'

'This is a nice place,' said Nobby, gazing around the shop. 'I like it here. There's always something happening; lots of people coming and going all the time. Lovely curtains, too. They look very tasty,' and to the animals' amazement, he leaned out and started to nibble a corner of fabric.

'Don't do that,' said Mulvey. 'Emily will be very upset if she comes in tomorrow morning to find her curtains all chewed up.'

'Stop it right this minute, Nobby. How many times have I told you to behave yourself?' the sheep said.

'Sorry. I couldn't help it. They looked delicious.' He looked so shame-faced that the other animals felt sorry for him, even Nora.

'You're right about this being a nice place, though,' she said to cheer him up a bit. 'Beats being down on the farm, eh Nobby?'

'I'll say.'

'What's it like being a farm animal?' asked Noreen. 'I've often wondered. I suppose it must be marvellous, all that freedom and fresh air.'

Nobby and Nora looked at each other. 'Shall we tell them?' said the sheep, and the goat nodded. And then to the astonishment of all the other animals, they began to chant at the tops of their voices, 'BOR-ING! BOR-ING! BOR-ING!'

'That's what it's like living on a farm,' Nobby said.

'Standing in a field all day, and more often than not it's raining,' Nora added. 'Nothing happens out on the hillside, and there's no one around except other sheep. And even though I'm one myself I have to admit they're the dullest creatures on earth. No sense of humour, no conversation, no imagination. There were days when I thought, "If I hear one more *Baa*, just one, I'll go mad." It had got to the point that I even looked forward to being sheared every year. It's quite uncomfortable, and you can feel a bit chilly afterwards with no fleece, but at least it's a bit of excitement.'

'I didn't even have that to look forward to.' said Nobby. 'No, believe you me, being in a pet shop is a thousand times better than being on a farm.'

'And by this time tomorrow, you'll be living in a castle. How much fun will that be?' said Mulvey. 'I wish there was a way we could know how you're getting on,' and he began to look very thoughtful. Strolling over to where the white mice lived he said, 'I think we need a volunteer. You'll do nicely, Willy.' The cat's paw darted out and whipped the mouse from its nest.

'No, no, I don't want to!' Willy squeaked. 'Put me back immediately.'

'Ooh, cheeky, aren't we? Giving orders. Anyway where's your sense of adventure? You don't even know what you're saying no to.'

'None of us do,' said Captain Cockle. 'What's your plan, Mulvey?'

'What we need,' replied the cat, 'is someone to go with Nobby and Nora and report back to us on what's happening. And you, Willy my old friend, are that special someone. Just watch this, everybody.' He hopped up on to one of the bales of hay and set the mouse down on the sheep's back. 'Now you see him...' and there was Willy, looking sulky and cross, '...and now you don't.' As the cat spoke, he leaned over and ruffled up the sheep's fleece, which was soft and thick. In an instant Willy was buried deep within it and had disappeared from sight. 'Clever or what?'

'Brilliant!' said Bubbles. 'How do you do it, that's what I want to know.'

'Sheer genius,' replied Mulvey.

Deep in the sheep's fleece something stirred and a tiny head popped out. 'How am I going to get back here afterwards, eh?' Willy squeaked. 'Have you worked that out yet, clever-clogs?'

'I have, of course. Presto will bring you back by magic.'

'Presto! Are you out of your mind? Don't you remember the last time? I'll end up lost in the middle of the night all on my own. I'll never find my way back here.'

'That wasn't my fault,' said Presto. 'It was Mulvey doing the magic that time, not me. Don't worry, Willy, I'll bring you home again, safe and sound.'

'When?'

They could see that the mouse was beginning to weaken.

'You'll only be gone for a day. I'll bring you home again tomorrow night at midnight and that's a promise.'

Willy thought about this for a moment. 'What about Emily? She'll notice that I'm not here.'

'She'll think that you're off visiting Martin.'

Martin was an old, sweet-natured, fat, brown house mouse, who lived in a hole in the skirting board. He was timid and shy and never came out, but everybody, even Emily, knew he was there and she knew too that the white mice went to stay with him from time to time.

'It could be great fun, Willy,' Bubbles argued. 'You'll probably never get the chance ever again to spend a day in a castle.'

'Oh all right then, I'll go. But you'll bring me back tomorrow night?'

'At the stroke of midnight. Don't worry, Willy,' said Presto. 'I won't let you down. Good luck.'

Ryan

The following morning, just after Finbarr had collected Nobby the goat and Nora the sheep (and, although he didn't realise it, Willy the white mouse too), Keira took Bubbles out for a walk. Ever since Mulvey, Bubbles and Captain Cockle had come back to the shop, Emily had wanted them to settle into their old routine, and so Keira and Bubbles set out for the holey stone. Bubbles, who was such a tiny scrap of a dog, pulled and tugged on the lead, alert to everything around her, paying attention to her surroundings like never before. It was a sparkling summer morning and when they reached the stone they sat down in the bright sunshine.

'I'll make a daisy chain for you, Bubbles. Would you like that?' Keira started to pick flowers. How surprised would she have been to learn that the last time the little yorkie had been to the stone was not with her, but with Mulvey and Captain Cockle, in the middle of a moonlit night!

'Hello. Do you mind if I join you?' said a tiny voice.

'Hello Ryan! How nice to see you, come and sit beside us.'

'Those animals are arriving at our place this morning so I wanted to be out. A sheep and a goat! Did you ever hear anything more silly in all your life. I thought I would burst out laughing in the shop yesterday.'

'I know,' said Keira. 'I saw you.'

'Mummy's always doing silly things like that. It embarrasses me. She thinks that the biggest thing has to be the best, and everybody else knows that's nonsense. That's why she bought the castle.'

'Isn't it fun living there?' asked Keira.

'I don't like it at all,' said Ryan. 'It's far too big. It's always cold, even on a beautiful day like this, and it feels lonely with just the two of us there in all those rooms. I don't know why Mummy can't see that we'd be better off in a smaller house, somewhere like that pretty cottage with all the ivy growing on it, the one opposite the orchard. Every time I pass it I think how cosy it looks and how nice it must be to live there.'

'That's Auntie Emily's house. That's where I'm staying for the summer.'

'Oh you lucky thing,' cried Ryan. 'And you get to work in the pet shop too, with all those animals. Tell me, has anyone bought the white rabbit yet?'

'No,' replied Keira, 'Presto's still there.'

'And the marmalade kittens?'

'Nobody's bought them either.'

'I think they're great, and I don't care what Mummy says, I bet they'll be lovely when they're grown up too.'

Keira had finished making her daisy chain. 'Come here, Bubbles.' She draped it around the little dog's neck and both she and Ryan laughed to see how delightful it looked. 'Bubbles is so happy to see you again,' Keira said. 'She hasn't stopped wagging her tail since you arrived.'

As if to prove that what Keira said was true, Bubbles leaned over and gently licked Ryan's hand.

'She's a wonderful dog and Bubbles is exactly the right name for her. I loved having her and the other animals in the castle and I do miss them. But when I think of all the nonsense they had to put up with, I'm not surprised they ran away. I just don't know how they managed to escape from the castle.'

'And I don't know how they ever managed to get back into the shop in the middle of the night. It's a real mystery.'

Bubbles started to bark, with such energy and force that she bounced up and down on the grass. 'You'd tell us if you could, wouldn't you?' Keira said, and the dog barked even louder. Ryan and Keira laughed again.

'I'd best be getting back to the shop. There's always a lot to do there.'

'And I suppose I'd better go home to see what's happening. Goodbye Keira, it's been so nice to talk to you,' Ryan said in his tiny voice. 'See you again soon, I hope. Bye-bye, Bubbles.'

'Goodbye Ryan! Goodbye!' And the little dog barked farewell.

Midnight

Everything went according to plan. Keira noticed that one of the white mice was missing, but Emily explained it away exactly as Mulvey had predicted, by saying that Willy must have gone into the mouse-hole in the skirting board as he sometimes did.

It was a relief to the animals when tea-time came and Keira and Emily closed up the shop. They all stayed up late that night, counting the dings of the angels' bells and waiting for midnight. Every hour seemed twice as long as the hour before: IIX, IX, X and XI.

'Gather round, everybody!' cried Presto as midnight approached. 'Get in a circle, but leave a clear space for Willy to land in.' The tension grew as they waited in silence for the bells. Bubbles was so nervous she started to giggle, but stopped when she noticed Mulvey glaring at her. Still they waited in absolute silence and then: *Ding! Ding! Ding!* As they counted the chimes, Presto closed his eyes. They could see that he was concentrating really hard. His brow was furrowed and his nose twitched faster than ever before.

Ding!

The final bell. Presto began to mutter under his breath and then cried aloud, 'ABRACADABRA!' And with that, Willy appeared.

He was in the space that had been left for him and he was lying on the flat of his back with his eyes closed.

'Willy! Willy?'

He didn't move. All the animals looked at each other.

'Willy?' Presto said again.

Still no reply. What could possibly have gone wrong? Now that the chimes had stopped there was once again silence in the shop. But wait a moment: not total silence. There was one very faint noise, a tiny whistling, wheezing sound. Mulvey noticed it before anyone else. Thanks to his splendid ears, he had excellent hearing.

'I know what that is!' he exclaimed. 'It's the sound of a mouse snoring. He's asleep, the little rascal.'

As if to prove the point, Willy opened his mouth wide and gave a huge yawn, showing all his bright, pin-like teeth, then rolled over on his side and started snoring again.

'Wake up, Willy,' Mulvey said, and he jabbed him with his paw.

'Aaaargh! Wassit? Where am I? What's

happening?' The mouse could hardly believe that he was already back in the shop. He told them that he had settled down early that evening in a quiet corner of the castle to wait for Presto to bring him home. 'I must have nodded off.'

'You're not telling me that you slept the whole way through the journey?' said Captain Cockle, who still hadn't quite recovered from his own scary trip.

'I suppose I must have. I can't remember anything about it. Oh but I've had the most marvellous time, I can't begin to tell you. Will you send me back again sometime, please, Presto? I so want to go back. You'll never believe who I met,' he went on, speaking now to the other white mice. 'Fergal! You know, Martin's long-lost brother? Poor Martin's wondered for years where he is and I'll be able to tell him now that Fergal's alive and well and living in the castle, as fat and fine a brown house mouse as ever you saw. Oh, by the way, he asked me to send you his best regards,' he said to Mulvey.

'Thanks,' said the cat shortly. He was actually mortified to have a house mouse sending him good wishes, particularly in front of Alexander and Aloysius. It just wasn't done for cats to get too pally with mice and he hoped they would never find out the circumstances of his meeting Fergal in the castle.

With that, Betty said 'How come you know Fergal, Mulvey? You never told us you met a mouse when you were there.'

To his relief, Willy butted in again before he could reply, pleading once more with Presto to send him back to the castle, this time perhaps with Billy or Milly as a companion. 'A long weekend would be just perfect.'

'You seem to be forgetting that I'm a magician's rabbit, not a travel agent,' Presto said haughtily. 'Long weekend indeed!' But the little mouse looked so disappointed at this and Presto was such a kindly creature that he immediately relented. 'We'll talk about this again later, Willy,' he said. 'We'll see what we can do.'

'But what about Nobby and Nora?' said Bubbles. 'That was the whole point of sending you there in the first place, so that you could report back to us.'

Willy started to laugh. 'It was hilarious,' he said. 'You've never seen anything funnier in all your life!'

'Tell us! Tell us!'

'Let him have something to eat and drink first,' squeaked one of the other mice. 'We saved you some grain, Willy, and here's a dish of clean water.'

'That's really kind of you, but honestly, I couldn't manage a single bite. I don't think I've ever eaten so much in my whole life as I have in the past day.' The animals looked at each other in astonishment. 'This is what happened. Gather round,' said the mouse.

And this is what he told them.

Henrietta's New Pets

Henrietta, with her trailing shawls and silver bracelets, met them at the door.

'Ooh, yum yum!' Nobby said as soon as he saw what she was wearing, although of course all Henrietta could hear was a bleat. He also noticed the faded rugs and the mouldy tapestries hanging on the wall, and his yellow eyes gleamed with delight.

Finbarr handed Mrs Fysshe-Pye two collars and leads.

'What are these for?'

'Sheep and goats need exercise,' he said. 'They're used to running about on the hills all day, not to being cooped up. And of course,' he went on, 'what's the point of having glamorous pets like these if no one can see them? Just think how impressed everyone will be when you walk down the street.'

As soon as Finbarr had gone, Nobby leaned over and started to nibble the end of one of Henrietta's shawls. 'Don't be naughty,' she said, pushing him away gently. But the shawl was made of silk and was one of the most delicious things Nobby had ever eaten. He couldn't resist taking another mouthful.

'Stop it!' She pushed him away again, quite roughly this time. 'You're to behave yourselves here. Now follow me.'

Nobby and Nora, with Willy still hidden in Nora's fleece, obediently followed Mrs Fysshe-Pye down the long, long hall and into the drawing room.

There was a fire blazing in the hearth and the sheep and goat immediately sat down in front of it.

'Hmm, that's better. They look more substantial than the last animals. They're the right size if nothing else.'

'This is brilliant!' Nora said. 'I'm really going to enjoy living here,' although Henrietta understood nothing of this, heard only a gentle *baa*.

What with the fleece and the fire, Willy had started to get quite hot and uncomfortable. Suddenly the phone rang in a distant corner of the castle. While Henrietta went off to answer it, Willie climbed down from the sheep's back. He was stiff as well as overheated, because mice are used to scampering about all the time and he was fed up with being stuck in the fleece, unable to move. It was then, he admitted, that he'd noticed the mouse hole in the wood panelling.

If you are a human being and you go to

a new place where you know no one, you can't just knock on the first door you come to and expect to be given a warm welcome, to be fed and looked after. But if you are a mouse, you will always be taken in by another mouse, be you white, black, brown or grey.

Fergal was delighted to meet Willy and when he realised that he was a friend of Martin, he insisted on bringing out a large piece of old and particularly smelly blue cheese that he had been keeping safe for just such a special occasion as this. They ate their fill. Fergal was urging Willy to have some more and Willy was saying that he couldn't eat another bite, not a crumb, when suddenly they heard a terrible screeching noise out in the drawing room. Excusing himself to Fergal and promising to call back later, Willy popped out of the mouse hole again to see what was happening.

Henrietta was standing in the middle of the floor screaming. Her face had gone a funny purple colour. Nora was standing in a corner of the room looking sullen and all over the rug were strange things like little black marbles.

'Sheep poo!' Henrietta screeched. 'Sheep poo all over my beautiful expensive Persian carpet! You wretched animal, how dare you.'

'How was I to know?' Nora said. 'When I'm out on the hillside I just go when I feel like it. Nobody told me that it was different in a castle.'

'And stop that horrible *baa*-ing noise. It's beginning to get on my nerves. Fresh air, that's what you need. I'll take you out for a walk like that man suggested.'

She put a collar and lead on poor Nora who was ever so annoyed and embarrassed about what had happened. As Mrs Fysshe-Pye struggled to do the same to Nobby – and it was a struggle, for Nobby didn't like the idea of a collar and lead, not one little bit – Willy crept back into the sheep's fleece.

As they were about to leave, the great front

door of the castle creaked open.

'Ah, there you are, Ryan. I'm just about to take these beasties for a walk. Come with us. I'll take the goat and you take the sheep.'

'But Mummy, I've just been out for a long walk already. I've been the whole way to the holey stone. I was going to read for a while.'

'Do as you're told. Goodness me, I don't know what's happened to you since you came to live in this town. You've become so disobedient and sullen, and I won't put up with it Ryan, do you hear?' She thrust the sheep's lead into her son's hands. 'Now follow me.'

But it was Nobby, not Henrietta, who led the way. Hugely excited by the prospect of a walk through town, he could wait no longer, and he shot out through the door of the castle, fast as a motor-boat, with Mrs Fysshe-Pye dragged like a water-skier behind him.

Walkies

High against the blue sky, the wind-vane glittered in the sunshine. Willy's heart thrilled within him as he gazed up at the great golden fish, at the castle's turrets and strange pointed windows. The little mouse had never been out and about in Gillnacurry before and everything he saw interested and delighted him. It was tremendous fun to be taken down the street hidden in Nora's fleece, peeking out at all the houses painted in such pretty colours, yellow and pink and cream.

Nobby was also having a great time. He stopped to chomp on a few red roses that were growing around someone's door, then suddenly darted off again towards a shop on the other side of the road, still dragging Mrs Fysshe-Pye behind him. The shop sold baskets of every shape and description, and a display of them was neatly arranged outside on the pavement to attract passers-by. Nobby had eaten two of the most dainty baskets and was getting stuck into a third when the shopkeeper shot out, in a fine old temper.

'How dare you! Who d'you think you are, Missus, letting your goat scoff my baskets? You'll pay me their full price, see if you don't.'

But before the man could say how much the baskets cost, Nobby was off again, this time towards a woman wearing what appeared to him a most scrumptious looking jacket. She screamed and took to her heels, and who can blame her? If a goat with a tremendous set of horns ran down the street towards you, planning to eat your clothes, I bet you'd get out of its way sharpish.

While all this was going on, Ryan and Nora were still trotting along calmly, with Willy peeping out from the fleece. But the mouse was so fascinated by everything he saw – such shops! such gardens! – that he forgot to stay carefully hidden.

And Ryan saw him.

The little boy gave a gentle tug on the lead and Nora stood still. He didn't say anything but he stared down at the mouse, who could feel himself being looked at. Willy almost fainted from sheer terror. His heart was beating so loudly he thought that Ryan must surely hear it, and he could do nothing, absolutely nothing but stare up, petrified, into the child's clear blue eyes.

Ryan stared back. He didn't speak. He didn't move. And then after what seemed like hours to Willy but was actually only a few moments,

Ryan said in his small, soft voice, 'Hello, mouse. How are you?' Willy didn't answer him. He was still frozen in fright. 'Are you all right in there? I imagine it must be so cosy sitting in the middle of a sheep's fleece.' Slowly and very cautiously, still gazing up into the little boy's eyes, Willy nodded his head. The child smiled. 'Well, hold tight and enjoy the rest of the journey. We'd better make a move.' He gently tugged the lead again and Nora set off once more, with her tiny passenger still on board.

Rounding the corner, they caught up with Henrietta and Nobby who were going more slowly now, for Nobby had worn himself out running around.

'Look at that silly woman,' a man said to his friend. 'Taking a goat for a walk on a lead. Really, some people will do absolutely anything to get attention.'

Henrietta went pink, but kept walking.

'Mum! Mum! Look!' a small girl cried. 'That lady must be barmy, having a pet goat and taking it out for walks.'

Still Henrietta said nothing but when, a few moments later, three builders saw her with Nobby and laughed so much they almost fell off their scaffolding, she turned to Ryan. 'It's your turn to take the goat for a while. Give me the sheep.'

'But Mummy...'

'No "buts", Ryan.' She took Nora's lead from his hands and put him in charge of Nobby.

On they went, into the centre of town, where they passed a shop selling nothing but cheese. Willy would never have imagined that there could be such a marvellous place. And then Nora saw something that that she found every bit as thrilling. 'Winnie's Wools' read the sign over the door, a door through which Nora ran as fast as her hooves could take her, dragging Henrietta along behind her.

'Wool! Wool!' Nora cried, standing in the middle of the shop floor. 'You have no idea how proud this makes me. Look at it! All the colours of the rainbow! Warm and soft! And every last little scrap of it comes from a sheep!'

'What's that creature doing in my shop?' said Winnie. 'Tell it to stop making that horrible *baa*-ing noise, and get it out of here, pronto.'

Henrietta tugged hard on the lead, which annoyed Nora. She pulled away and bumped into a shelf laden with wool, which fell down just as Ryan and Nobby came through the door.

'Your sheep's wrecking my shop! And now there's a goat too!' Winnie screamed, as dozens and dozens of balls of wool, red and yellow and blue, tumbled to the floor.

'Yum-bags scrum-bags,' said Nobby, and three balls of wool vanished as fast as if he were a child eating wine-gums. 'The orange one was the best. I wonder what the green ones taste like?' And he tucked in once more.

'Wool! Wool!' Nora cried again. 'Where would you humans be without us sheep? You'd have no blankets or jumpers, no cardigans or socks. You'd have frozen toes and chilly fingers. Wool! Wool!'

'Get those beasts out of here! Now!'

As she dashed around in the middle of all this hullabaloo, Nora knocked over another shelf. Poor Willy, who had been holding on for dear life, suddenly lost his grip on the fleece and tumbled to the floor.

Oh no!

And then Mrs Fysshe-Pye saw him.

'ARRRGH! A MOUSE! A MOUSE!'

Immediately, Ryan scooped Willy up in his hand and hid him in his pocket. 'There's no mouse here, Mummy. You must have imagined it.'

'There is,' Henrietta insisted. 'I saw it. Here this woman is complaining about my animals when her own shop is infested with vermin.'

Vermin! There's no worse insult to a mouse, and Willy was so cross he almost popped out of Ryan's pocket to give Henrietta a piece of his mind. But he didn't need to: Winnie was every bit as furious.

'There are no mice in my shop!' she screeched.

'Are!'

'Aren't!'

'Please, Mummy...'

'*Baa!*'

'I wonder if a hank of wool is tastier than a ball of wool?'

'Get out of here! Get out of here or I'll call the police!'

'Wool! Wool!'

With great difficulty, Ryan managed to coax Nora and Nobby out onto the street. He slipped Willy back into the sheep's fleece for the journey home just as Winnie turfed Henrietta out of the shop.

'And don't come back!' she bellowed after them.

More Trouble

Bone-weary, they returned to the castle, where Henrietta took a great iron key from her pocket to open the door. Glancing down, she saw on the step a few of the familiar black marbles. She started to scream as she realised that there were more of them, lots more, the whole way across the drawbridge.

'That horrible sheep! It's done it again! First it poos all over my carpet and then all over my step and drawbridge!'

'Oh for goodness sake!' exclaimed Nora. 'There's just no pleasing some people. She didn't like it when I went in the castle, so I decided I'd better go outside this time, and now she's annoyed about that too. What AM I supposed to do? Is there some kind of special sheep toilet around here that I just haven't noticed? I don't think so.'

After a great deal of fuss, they all finally went into the castle again. It was a huge relief to Willy to sneak back through the mouse hole to visit Fergal once more. This time, Fergal lit two tiny flares and led him down a long, long, dark, winding tunnel until they came to...the larder.

Willy's eyes grew round with amazement as he gazed at all the food stored there. Whole cheeses! Chocolate biscuits! And what was that strange and wonderful, rather wobbly-looking thing over there on the white plate?

'Jelly. Lemon jelly,' Fergal said, helpful as always. 'It's difficult to carry things back through the tunnel, so eat as much as you want while you're here. Tuck in!'

Much later, their tummies plump with goodies, the two mice toddled back through the tunnel to Fergal's home, where they sat talking for a long time about Martin and the pet shop; and also about many other things that would be of interest only to mice. At last Willy said goodbye. He thanked Fergal for everything and promised that if it were at all possible, he would come back some day to visit him again. Then he went back out into the drawing room to see what was happening.

Nobby had also had a fine meal, for he had eaten several of the tapestries hanging on the walls. 'I don't know what it is that makes them so tasty. Maybe it's all the dust.'

Nora climbed onto Henrietta's lap and sat down. 'Isn't this one of the things pets are supposed to do? It's ever so uncomfortable. This woman's knees are terribly bony.' Ryan came into the room and could hardly see his mother, hidden as she was behind the great bulk of Nora's fleece. He did his best not to giggle.

'Gerroff! Stoppit!' said Mrs Fysshe-Pye as Nora fidgeted, trying to make herself comfy. 'And let me tell you this – you and that goat are going back to where you came from, first thing tomorrow morning.'

'HOORAY!' Nora and Nobby cried together.

'I never thought I'd hear myself say this, but I can't wait to see my farmer again,' said Nobby.

'I'll even be glad to see his sheep-dog,' added Nora. 'Life was much better out there on the hillside than I realised at the time. I'll never grumble about it ever, ever again.'

It was at this point that Willy noticed the time. It was later than he had thought. He wanted to be ready for the trip home, about which he was rather nervous, given what Mulvey and the others had told him. He went behind the sideboard to wait for Presto to say the magic words. Worn out with all the excitement, he fell fast asleep there, and when he woke up, he was back in the pet shop, at the end of what would have been for anyone, let alone a little white mouse, a truly extraordinary day.

Finbarr in Love

In his long, skinny bed in his tall, skinny house, Finbarr awoke. 'I'mnotgoingtoseeEmily today,' was his first sleepy thought. 'I'mnotgoingtoseeEmilytodayI'mnotgoingtos eeEmilytodayI'mnotgoingtoseeEmilytoday.' And then suddenly his brain switched on fully, and he realised the meaning of what he had been thinking. He poked his nose out over the blankets and wailed aloud, 'I'M NOT GOING TO SEE EMILY TODAY!'

He crawled out of his bed and got washed and dressed, then went downstairs. Over breakfast, he thought about yesterday. He'd been delivering pet food to the shop when that woman with the big long name he could never remember had marched into the place. She'd been in a right old strop, complaining about the sheep and the goat. Finbarr had promised that he would go to the castle and take them away that very afternoon. But he had also promised that he would get more big pets for the woman, suitable ones this time.

'It's your last chance to prove this really is a proper pet shop,' Mrs Wotsit had said, glaring at Emily. 'And as for you,' she'd continued, turning her weird round eyes on Finbarr, 'don't show up at my door with an elephant, because I don't want one. Nor a lion. Nor a giraffe.'

'I wouldn't dream of it,' Finbarr had said. This was a fib. Even as the woman was talking, he'd been planning to go straight round to

Gillnacurry zoo to see if there were any big animals on sale there.

As soon as Her Ladyship had stomped off, Emily had sighed and said, 'Thank you so much for promising to help me with this, because I really haven't a clue what to do next.'

The problem was, neither had Finbarr.

To make matters worse, Emily had added, 'You needn't come to the shop tomorrow. Take the day off and enjoy yourself. I've given you so much trouble lately.'

'It's no trouble! No trouble at all!'

But Emily had insisted. 'I don't want to see you back here until the day after tomorrow.'

And so the whole, empty Emilyless day stretched before him. What would he do to make it pass more quickly? He decided to go for a walk up to the holey stone, and on the way he would have a think about what could be done to get hold of some big animals.

The walk turned out to be a good idea, for it was such a fine summer morning that

Finbarr couldn't feel miserable for long, as he walked through the bright streets of Gillnacurry. He perked up even more when he reached the holey stone itself and found Keira and Bubbles sitting there.

'Hello Finbarr! How are you? How did you get on yesterday afternoon? Did you collect the sheep and the goat and take them back to your brother's farm?'

'I did. It was amazing. As soon as we let them out into the field the goat started doing cartwheels and the sheep started dancing with the sheep-dog. My brother Davy's been a farmer for ages and he said he'd never seen anything like it before in his whole life.'

'Auntie Emily's very grateful to you for helping her. She said yesterday after you'd left the shop, "Finbarr's so thoughtful and kind, I don't know what I'd do without him."'

'Did she really?' he cried. 'Did Emily say that about me?'

Keira nodded. They sat in silence for some

moments as he thought about this. Bubbles watched them both with her bright, intelligent eyes and Keira stroked her head, little imagining just how closely the dog was following all they said.

'Do you know what this stone is for, Finbarr?' Keira asked eventually. 'I come here every morning and I always wonder about it.'

'There are all sorts of ideas. Some people think it was for getting married. I mean, say someone like me had lived in Gillnacurry more than a thousand years ago, and he'd wanted to get married to someone, say someone like Emily. Then they'd have come here. And she'd have put her hand through the hole in the stone and he, he'd have held her hand in his, and they'd have said some words, special words. And then, why then they'd have been married.' As he told Keira this Finbarr's voice had grown soft and his face seemed to glow with delight at the very thought of someone like him marrying someone like Emily over a thousand years ago.

'Finbarr, you're really fond of Auntie Emily, aren't you?'

He felt his face go hot and red and he nodded. 'Who told you that? How did you know?'

'I just guessed. You should tell her,' Keira said.

'Oh I couldn't!'

'Of course you could.'

'I couldn't.'

'You could.' But he looked so miserable now that Keira felt sorry for him and decided not to insist any more. 'Anyway, like I said, she's very fond of you.'

'And I will get some big animals for her,' Finbarr cried. 'I promised her and I won't let her down. I don't know how I'll do it but I will. Just see if I don't!'

Some Enormous Animals

In all her years of working with animals, Emily had seen some strange sights. She had seen a bald cat. She had seen a poodle with a Mohican haircut and a rabbit with a curly coat. But never in all her life had she seen or even dreamed of creatures like those that Finbarr brought to her shop the following afternoon.

'This is Snowdrop,' he said, 'and this is Feathers.'

Snowdrop was a white cat with green eyes and Feathers was a yellow budgie. They were like any common-or-garden cat or budgie but for one significant detail: they were simply ENORMOUS.

Feathers was perched on Finbarr's outstretched arm.

'It's as big as an eagle,' Emily murmured.

'Bigger,' Keira said. 'Much bigger.'

Snowdrop was sitting at Finbarr's feet, and the points of her ears were level with his waist (and Finbarr, as you are well aware, was not a short man).

'It's as big as me,' Keira whispered.

'Bigger,' Emily said. 'Much bigger.'

The huge cat gazed around. Its green eyes were cold and unfriendly. And then suddenly, without any warning whatsoever, it gave a horrible blood-curdling mew, and sprang across the floor of the shop, heading straight for Mulvey's basket! Clearly terrified, Mulvey jumped out. It was just as well he did, otherwise he would have been crushed beneath Snowdrop's enormous great bum. While Mulvey cowered over by the window, the white cat climbed into his beloved basket as if she had every right to be there.

It was a tight fit. The sides of the basket strained and groaned as Snowdrop forced her immense bulk into it. There was the sound of wicker snapping.

'You behave yourself!' Finbarr cried. 'That's Mulvey's basket, not yours. Come on, scram! Hoppit.'

But the big cat didn't budge.

With that, the budgie took off. It flew across the shop to where Captain Cockle was sitting on his perch. The parrot wasn't giving in so easily. Bravely, it sat tight but POW! With a single blow of its wing the budgie sent poor Captain Cockle flying in a squawking riot of coloured feathers. But the budgie was too heavy for the perch. As soon as it sat down on it, it smashed into bits. With a nasty cackle,

Feathers swooped off again.

'Finbarr,' Emily said, 'I don't think this is going to work.'

And with that, *clang!* The shop door opened and in came Henrietta and Ryan. To Emily's amazement, Mrs Fysshe-Pye gave a huge smile when she saw the cat and the budgie.

'Now this is more like it!' she cried.

'No, Mummy,' Ryan whispered. 'Please Mummy, no. Don't do it, please!'

'But they're exactly what I want, you silly boy. They're pets and they're big. This is perfect.'

'Maybe this isn't a good idea,' Finbarr said. 'You might need, er, special training, or, um, a special licence.'

'I want them,' Henrietta said.

'It might be an idea to think about it first,' Emily said. 'Don't rush into things.'

'What's wrong with you people?' Mrs Fysshe-Pye said. 'As soon as you get something that's just what I want, you drag your feet about selling it to me. Now enough of this nonsense. Ryan, stop whimpering. Can you deliver them tomorrow?' she asked Finbarr.

'Why wait?' he said, realising there was no turning her. 'I'll bring them round right now.'

'Excellent!' Mrs Fysshe-Pye paid Emily, and then hustled Ryan, still protesting weakly, out of the shop so that they could hurry home and be there to meet Finbarr when he arrived.

It was a struggle to catch Feathers, whose wings made a strong wind as he flew around the shop.

'Why can't you be like the cat?' Finbarr cried. 'Look how well behaved she is.'

Snowdrop was now sitting beside the door with her paws together and her tail curled neatly around them, all ready to leave. The cat smiled insincerely at Finbarr's words.

But what of all the other animals in the shop? For some strange reason they were behaving badly too. Noreen tried to climb out of her tank, a thing she had never done before.

Mulvey had climbed up the curtains and was making a nasty low, gurgling mewing sound, and even little Betty pushed her wheel over on its side, and turned her food bowl upside-down. At last Finbarr managed to catch the budgie, which half dragged him out to his own van. Snowdrop wandered out behind them.

'Now we can try to work out what's wrong with this lot,' Emily said, as a marmalade kitten flew past at eye-level, and Captain Cockle squawked madly. 'They're clearly trying to tell us something.'

'I think I know what it is, and it's not good news. Auntie Emily, Bubbles is missing.'

All the animals fell silent and still.

'Oh no!'

But Keira was right. The little yorkie was nowhere to be seen. They hunted all over the shop, in cupboards and boxes, everywhere.

'Could she have slipped out the door when Mrs Fysshe-Pye and Ryan came in?' asked

Keira.

'But this is her home,' replied Emily. 'Bubbles would never do a thing like that.'

'She might have done it because she was frightened by the big animals.'

And so they looked in the street and they asked in the neighbouring shops and houses, but there was no sign of Bubbles anywhere. Poor Emily was in tears by the time they returned to the shop. 'This is just terrible. Where on earth can she be?'

The answer to this question was extraordinary.

Snowdrop and Feathers

Bubbles was in Snowdrop's armpit. Yes, you read that correctly, but I'll repeat it so that there can be no doubt whatsoever. Bubbles was in Snowdrop's armpit. Deep in the cat's thick fur it was dark and unbearably hot. Just as Bubbles thought she was about to suffocate, the cat moved its paw and the dog dropped out onto the floor of Finbarr's van. 'Let's have a look at you, Titch,' she sneered.

'Please don't hurt me, Snowdrop.'

'Don't you "Snowdrop" me! I'm Buster.'

'And I'm Spike,' said Feathers.

'Great names. They – they suit you both,' the little dog stammered.

'Yeah, we know,' replied the budgie.

'I'm Bubbles,' said Bubbles, and the other two animals fell around laughing.

'What a dopey name!' snickered the cat.

'Why have you brought me here?'

'Why not? Stupid little scrap of a dog like you will never be missed.'

'Oh yes I will,' Bubbles said bravely. 'All my friends saw you kidnap me. They know what you did.'

'Big deal. Nothing they can do about it, is there?' the budgie replied.

With that, the van came to a halt.

'Seems like we've arrived.' The cat scooped the dog up in her paw and before Bubbles had a chance to say, 'Please don't put me in your armpit again,' Snowdrop did something far worse. She stuffed the poor creature into one of her pointed ears.

Finbarr opened the back doors of the van. Feathers/Spike climbed onto his arm while Snowdrop/Buster hopped out and minced up to the door of the castle. She smirked and Bubbles heard her whisper to the budgie, 'This is going to be a bit of fun!'

As well as delivering the animals, Finbarr had brought with him crates and crates of cat food and a mountain of bird seed.

'Why, there's enough here to last a month,' Henrietta said.

'You only think that, Missus,' Finbarr replied as he revved up the van. 'Wait till you see this pair tuck into their grub. Cheerio. And good luck!'

'Isn't this splendid!' Henrietta said to Ryan as they stood in the drawing room. It has to be said that the big animals did fit in. They suited the size of the castle and looked as if they belonged there as the small animals and the farm animals had not.

Snowdrop was finding it a bit itchy and irritating having a dog stuck in her ear. Suddenly it became too much to bear. She twitched her head and Bubbles tumbled out onto the carpet. Dazed and stunned as she was, the little yorkie knew what she had to do: RUN! She belted across the carpet with the cat after her.

'EEEK! A MOUSE! A MOUSE!'

'No it's not, it's Bubbles!'

'Don't talk nonsense, Ryan.'

'But it is, I saw her clearly. What on earth is she doing here?'

By now Bubbles was under the sideboard with her back pressed against the wall. She watched in horror as a great white paw with glinting claws swept back and forth in front of her.

'I'm telling you, Ryan, it was a mouse. A horrible fat brown mouse. I saw it as it ran.'

The paw withdrew and Bubbles heard the cat say, 'Mouse? There are mice here? Nobody told me that. I wouldn't have come here if I'd known there were mice.'

'Goodness, what a loud mew it has!'

'Scared, aren't ya?' That was the budgie.

'I am not.'

'Are too!'

'I – I just don't like them, that's all. I don't know what it is about them; they make me nervous.'

'Cowardly-custard cat! Cowardly-custard cat!'

'You shut your beak.'

'Perhaps we should give them their dinner now?' said Ryan.

Finbarr had been right about the food. The budgie guzzled seed until they thought it must surely explode. Although Henrietta opened tin after tin of cat food, she couldn't keep up with the rate at which the big cat ate. It became bad-tempered when there was a pause for a few moments while she struggled to open the umpteenth can. 'I shall have to get a new tin opener, perhaps an electric one. This one is much too slow...YEOW!' she shrieked, as an impatient Snowdrop sank her claws deep in her shins.

Having eaten so well themselves, did the animals then let Mrs Fysshe-Pye and Ryan have their dinner in peace? Not a bit of it. The cat snaffled Ryan's fish fingers from right under his nose and there was nothing he could do about it. Henrietta had some fresh pineapple but Feathers flew down and scoffed the lot before she even had a chance to pick up her knife and fork.

'The cheek of them! I don't like these beasties either. You'd think they owned the place!'

Things Turn Really Nasty

'"You'd think they owned the place." Now there's a thought,' said the cat. 'Imagine having your own castle.'

As it spoke, it put out its paw and touched the end of one of Henrietta's trailing scarves. 'Stop it! Leave me alone!'

But there was no stopping Snowdrop who, as Bubbles watched from her hiding place beneath the sideboard, unwound the scarf from Mrs Fysshe-Pye's neck. The budgie, meanwhile, had slit open a cushion and started to rummage through it. Great clouds of feathers flew into the air.

'Wonder if the sofa's the same. Let's find out.' Riiiiiipppp!

'Stop it, I tell you.'

'I don't like these animals at all. I'm frightened, Mummy.'

'There's no reason to be.'

But Mrs Fysshe-Pye was wrong. As she spoke, Feathers, who had been sitting on the back of the sofa, spread his mighty wings and took off. He swooped across the room to where Ryan was standing, and before the little boy could do anything to save himself, the budgie snatched him up! It dipped down, hooked its claws into his jumper and kept flying, with poor Ryan now dangling there, helpless and terrified.

'Ryan! My baby! Let him go, you big brute.'

The budgie carried on, straight out through the door of the room and up the hall.

Henrietta ran after the bird and Snowdrop ran after her. Bubbles ran after all of them to see what was happening.

Feathers flew effortlessly up the wide stone stairs, still carrying the unfortunate Ryan. Mrs Fysshe-Pye was now running partly to catch up with them and partly to escape the enormous cat, who was bounding along behind her.

'Help! Help!' Ryan cried.

'Don't worry, darling. Mummy's here.'

Now they were all racing along a passageway deep in the castle, past suits of armour, past spears and shields fixed to the walls. Poor Bubbles' tiny legs and paws were worn out with all the running. Just as the dog thought she was going to have to give up in exhaustion, Feathers flew through an open doorway.

The bird dumped Ryan on the floor and, without stopping, flew out of the room again. Henrietta ran in to where her son was lying in a heap.

'My poor baby! Are you all right?'

BOOM!

With that the stout wooden door of the room slammed shut behind them. They heard the sound of a bolt being drawn, and in dismay, Ryan and Henrietta realised that they were now prisoners in their own home.

A Big Surprise for Bubbles

The cat and the budgie lost no time at all in taking over the place. First, they went downstairs again and raided the pantry. Creeping behind them to see what they were up to, but still taking care to stay hidden, Bubbles listened at the pantry door. She could hear the smash and crash of bowls and dishes being over-turned, followed by loud, rude slurping and munching noises. Stuffed with food, the pair finally came out into the passageway again.

'That was delicious, Spike,' the cat said, and it gave a tremendous burp. 'Let's go back upstairs and have a poke around, see what we can find there.'

The first room they came to was all soft and frilly, with pink curtains and a heap of little cushions on the bed.

'This must be Mrs Fysshe-Pye's bedroom,' Bubbles thought, peeping around the door.

Snowdrop sat down at the dressing-table, which was covered in silver jewellery. The cat slipped its paw through a wide bracelet. 'Oh, I like this,' she murmured. She helped herself to another and then another, and admired her reflection in the mirror.

The budgie was interested in the pots and jars of makeup that were sitting on the dressing-table.

'Help me paint myself, Buster,' he said. 'I've always wanted to be lots of different colours, like that parrot we saw in the pet shop.'

'I will in a minute.' Snowdrop was now deep

in the drawer where Mrs Fysshe-Pye kept all her scarves. Choosing three of the most beautiful, she draped them around her neck. With her huge round eyes and trailing scarves, laden with silver jewellery that tinkled as she moved, the effect was very curious. If Henrietta had been turned by magic into a cat, she would have looked exactly like Snowdrop.

Smeared with blue and green eye-shadow, and with a blob of rouge on his breast, Feathers looked nothing like Captain Cockle, which was what he wanted more than anything. The place was beginning to look very untidy now, with scarves hanging out of half-opened drawers; with face-powder sprinkled all over the floor and lipstick smeared on the mirror. Even the cat admitted that it was a mess.

'What we need is a servant to clean up after us. I know! That stupid little dog we brought from the shop! She'd make the perfect maid. I wonder where she's got to?'

As soon as she heard this, Bubbles moved away from the door and scampered off down the stairs as fast as she could to get away from the gruesome twosome. Where might she hide? The drawing room, perhaps. They seemed intent on wrecking the castle room by room, and as Feathers had already torn up the sofa and cushions there it might be quite some time before they went back. And so Bubbles sneaked into the drawing-room again…only to get the surprise of her life!

Sitting in the middle of the hearth-rug were Noreen and the two marmalade kittens.

'What on earth are you doing here?'

'Presto sent us to bring you home,' said Alexander.

'We volunteered,' added Aloysius proudly. 'Most everyone in the shop said it would be really dangerous and that we were too little, but Mulvey backed us up. He said we were brave and would be well able for anything.'

'And then we all decided that a snake might

come in handy,' said Noreen, beaming. 'So here we are. But tell us, how have you been since last we saw you?'

And so Bubbles told them everything that had happened and they listened in shock.

'That poor little boy!' Alexander said when she had finished. 'We must help him if we can.'

'Oh please, yes,' said Bubbles. 'Ryan was always so good to Mulvey, Captain Cockle and me when we were here in the castle together. We can't just go away and leave him and his mother at the mercy of those terrible creatures.'

'We have plenty of time,' said Noreen. 'Presto thought it might be difficult for us to find you here, so he won't be bringing us home for hours yet.'

Aloysius looked very thoughtful. 'I'm sure we can do this,' he said. 'We must work out a plan. Has anyone got any ideas?'

'I don't know how this can be of use to us,' said Bubbles, 'but there is one thing that Snowdrop really doesn't like...'

Fergal

'So what we need is a mouse,' said Alexander. 'What a pity we didn't bring one with us.'

'That's just typical of them, isn't it? They're never around when you need them.'

Bubbles thought this was rather unfair of Aloysius.

'I'm sure one can be found though,' Alexander said, and he pointed to a little hole in the wood panelling.

'Yoo-hoo! Anyone home?' he called into the

mouse-hole. 'Don't be afraid, it's not what you think. We need your help.'

'A likely story!' squeaked a tiny voice. 'You must be thick if you imagine for one minute I'd fall for a line like that.'

Alexander and Aloysius looked at each other in delight. So there WAS a mouse in there. Now all they had to do was coax it out.

'Oldest trick in the book,' the little voice continued. 'My mum warned me about cats like you.'

'No, honestly, please. It's not a trick or a trap. It's just that we need a mouse.'

'I bet you do! Got some special recipe and all the ingredients bar one, eh?'

'We should have brought Willy instead of Noreen,' Aloysius grumbled. 'But how were we to know at the time?'

Suddenly the mouse went quiet. 'Willy?' the tiny voice squeaked after a very long pause. 'Did you say "Willy"?'

At this, Alexander had a brainwave. 'Why of

course! You must be Fergal!'

They could hear the mouse gasp in astonishment. 'How do you know my name?'

'Willy told us all about you.'

'Do you know Mulvey too?' By now the four friends could see the little mouse sitting in the shadows, just inside the mouse-hole.

'Mulvey and Willy are friends of ours. We all live together in the same pet shop.'

'So you do. They both told me about it.' All of a sudden, a brown snout popped out of the mouse hole. 'Mulvey's a remarkable cat,' Fergal said, unexpectedly. 'I was at his mercy. He could have eaten me up, but instead he helped me to escape. If you're his friends, I think I owe it to him to try to help you.'

He stepped right out of the mouse-hole, and for the first time they were all able to have a good look at each other. Poor Fergal! A yorkie, a snake and two frisky kittens is about as scary a line-up as any mouse could ever be expected to face, but he was a stout-hearted little fellow and did his best not to tremble. 'What exactly is it you want me to do?'

'You see, it's like this,' said Alexander. 'A budgie and a cat have taken over the castle, and we want you to help us catch the cat. It's afraid of mice, absolutely terrified of them. The only thing is, it's, um, rather a big cat.'

'How big?' asked the mouse.

There was no reply.

'How big?' Fergal asked again. 'I mean, is it as big as Mulvey?'

'Bigger,' Alexander whispered.

'Much, much bigger,' added Aloysius.

Fergal's eyes grew round with fright.

Bubbles took a deep breath. 'Do you know Ryan?' she asked, and the mouse nodded. 'Well, slightly bigger than him.'

Crump! That was the sound of Fergal fainting out cold on the floor. They lifted up his head and fanned him with their paws until he opened his eyes again.

'You cats! You don't ask for much, do you?'

he said sarcastically. 'And what about the budgie?'

'Leave him to me, sweetie,' said Noreen. 'I'll deal with him.'

In her heart, Bubbles felt sure that Fergal was just about to bolt back to his mouse-hole, never to come out again, when the mouse took a deep breath and said, 'All right, I'll do it. I'll do it for Willy and Mulvey. What's the plan?'

To the Rescue!

Meanwhile, over at the other side of town, in Emily's house, Keira couldn't sleep. She was very upset that they hadn't been able to find Bubbles, and couldn't stop thinking about what might be happening in the castle. At last she decided to go downstairs and have a drink of milk. As she approached the kitchen door, she was surprised to see that the light was already on.

Emily was sitting at the table with her head in her hands.

'Oh Keira,' she said, 'I'm worried sick. I should never have sold those animals to that woman.'

'But she wanted them.'

'It doesn't matter. I should have insisted and said no. That poor little boy! I do so hope he's all right.'

'Yes, poor Ryan,' Keira said.

'I'll never forgive myself if anything happens to him. What should we do?'

'Ring Finbarr.'

'But it's the middle of the night!' exclaimed Emily.

'Finbarr won't mind. I bet he's worried too and I know he'll do everything he can to help.'

He answered the phone on the very first ring. 'Ooh, I'm so glad it's you, Emily. I was afraid it might be Mrs Wotsit in the castle. It's putting me off my sleep, wondering how they are over there.'

'Me too. Finbarr, I'm so worried.'

'Do you want me to drive over and check

how they're getting on? I can collect you and Keira too if you like; we can all go.'

'Could you really do that?'

Finbarr told her that it would be no trouble at all.

Five minutes later the big blue lorry with its yellow slogan, FINBARR'S FEEDS, FOR YOUR ANIMAL'S NEEDS, pulled up at Emily's front door. It was driven by Finbarr, who was still in his stripy pyjamas. 'I rang the zoo,' he said, 'just to be on the safe side. They're going to send a couple of people over.'

Emily and Keira climbed into the cab and they sped off through the night-time streets of Gillnacurry.

Emily spoke only once during the short journey. 'Where did you get those monsters?' she said.

'I bought them on the internet!' he wailed. 'It seemed like a good idea at the time.'

There were lights on in the castle when they got there, and they were relieved to find that the great front door was unlocked. Finbarr pushed it open and they tip-toed inside, advanced fearfully up the long, long hallway.

'What a mess!' Emily said when they looked into the drawing room and saw the ruined sofa and cushions. But there was no one there and so they continued on. They came to the pantry, and it was also a disaster zone. There were broken dishes and spilled food everywhere, a horrible mixture of things: peas and corn-flakes and jelly and milk and sausages.

'It's just as well we came over,' Finbarr said. 'Things are every bit as bad as I feared.'

They went upstairs and came to Mrs Fysshe-Pye's bedroom, where bright scarves hung untidily from half-opened drawers and face powder had been spilt on the carpet. Coloured make-up was smeared and scattered all over the dressing table and mirror.

'But where are Henrietta and Ryan?' Keira said. 'And where are Snowdrop and Feathers?'

They all felt quite afraid now.

Suddenly, they could hear a noise in the distance, a thumping noise, a mad hullabaloo. It was coming from a room at the bottom of the corridor and they crept towards it, terrified of what they might find there. A little sign on the door announced that this was the library of the castle.

'I'll go first,' Finbarr said, and he cautiously turned the handle. He gasped at what he saw there, then flung the door wide so that Keira and Emily could also see.

The thumping noise they had heard was Snowdrop being chased around and around the room by...

'*A mouse!* And what is Bubbles doing here?' Emily cried. 'And the kittens too, look, look!'

Alexander and Aloysius were perched on top of a bookcase, while Feathers flapped around, squawking madly. He looked very strange, for he was smeared and smudged with rouge and eye-shadow, red and green and blue. Snowdrop also looked bizarre, for she was wearing loads of scarves and silver bracelets.

One of the kittens – was it Aloysius or Alexander? In the heat of the moment it was hard to tell – was standing on his back legs now, and was holding something in his right front paw, a long, dark straight thing.

'It's a javelin,' said Finbarr.

'No, it's not, it's a spear,' said Emily.

'No, it's not, it's...it's NOREEN!' cried Keira.

And she was right. As she spoke, the kitten started to run fast on its back legs along the top of the bookcase. Halfway along it let go of the snake and threw it forwards, as hard as it could. Still stiff as a spear, Noreen flew through the air, heading for the budgie. At that very moment, Snowdrop decided she could take no more. With a wild and miserable mew she made a flying leap towards Finbarr, who had the good sense to hold out his arms. He staggered and almost fell as he caught the enormous white cat, so heavy and hot with its thick white fur.

Noreen hit Feathers in full flight, smack in the middle of his painted breast. Immediately she went limp as a rope and swung round and round the budgie, pinning its wings to its side. The big bird fell to the floor, tied up like a package all ready for the post.

'Zoo! Zoo!' cried a voice suddenly from deep within the castle. 'We're here from the zoo! Where are you?'

'Up here, come quickly, quickly! Help!' Emily shouted.

In a few minutes, it was all over. The zoo men scooped Snowdrop out of Finbarr's arms and into a net. They unwound Noreen from around Feathers and put the bird in a cage. They were going to take Noreen away too, but Emily stopped them just in time. 'The snake is mine,' she said. 'The snake and the kittens and the dog.' The mouse had simply disappeared.

'But where,' said Keira, as the zoo men went off with the two monstrous animals, 'where are Ryan and Henrietta?'

Ryan and Finbarr Speak Out

They went through the castle, looking into empty rooms and calling out until at last they heard a banging noise from behind a bolted door.

'We're in here! Help! Help! Let us out.'

Emily drew back the bolt and opened the door, to be met by Ryan and his mother. Mrs Fysshe-Pye was so angry that her face had gone a funny purple colour and she grabbed Finbarr by the collar of his pyjamas. 'There ought to be a law against people like you!' she yelled. 'You're a disgrace! You listen to me, you fool.' But before she could say another word, something extraordinary happened.

Ryan spoke up, and not in his usual tiny little voice, but in a loud, loud roar that made their ears ring. 'NO! It's not Finbarr's fault, Mummy, it's YOURS!' he bellowed like an elephant. 'Emily didn't want to sell those animals to you but you made her do it, you insisted. She warned you, and Finbarr too, but you didn't listen. You don't listen, not ever, NEVER. When you bought the castle everybody told you it was too big, even the man who owned it, but you went ahead and bought it anyway. Mulvey and Bubbles and Captain Cockle were perfectly nice pets, it was the castle that was all wrong, and anyway, you were horrible to them. Anybody could see that it was daft to have a pet sheep and a goat, but not you.'

'Oh Ryan!' Henrietta whimpered.

'Mummy,' he said, 'you *are* my mummy and

I do so love you, but sometimes you make mistakes.'

'We all do,' said Finbarr.

'Sometimes small things are better than big things. There's no *need* to try and impress people.'

By now Mrs Fysshe-Pye was very upset. Emily passed her a hankie and she wiped her eyes, blew her nose. 'I'm sorry, Ryan,' she sobbed. 'You're right. I've been so selfish. I only thought about what I wanted and I didn't listen to anyone else. I put us both in danger with those creatures but I promise you, it'll never happen again. I'll change my ways from this very night.'

'I didn't want to shout at you Mummy, but I couldn't see any other way.'

Henrietta put her arms around Ryan and gave him a great big hug and a kiss.

'Perhaps we should all go home,' Emily said. 'You must be worn out after all you've been through; I'm sure you both want to sleep.'

'Before we go,' Finbarr replied, 'there's something I want to say too, something, like Ryan, that I've wanted to say for a long, long time and I don't think it can wait a minute longer.'

'And what is that?'

Finbarr took a deep breath and he said very quietly, 'IloveyouEmilyIloveyouEmilyIloveyou Emily,' and then he shouted aloud at the top of his voice, 'I LOVE YOU EMILY!'

Emily went pink with surprise and delight. 'Ooh, thanks for telling me, Finbarr. I love you too.'

'Do you? Do you really?'

She nodded in reply.

'Will you come and live with me forever? Emily, will you marry me?'

And Emily of course said…

'Yes.'

A Most Remarkable Wedding

In his long, skinny bed in his tall, skinny house, Finbarr awoke. 'I'mgoingtogetmarriedtoEmily today,' was his first sleepy thought. 'I'mgoingto getmarriedtoEmilytodayI'mgoingtogetmarried toEmilytodayI'mgoingtogetmarriedtoEmily today.' And then suddenly his brain switched on fully and he realised the meaning of what he had been thinking. He sat bolt upright and he shouted aloud, 'I'M GOING TO GET MARRIED TO EMILY TODAY!'

He jumped out of bed and raced upstairs to the bathroom. It was only after he got out of the shower that he realised that he'd forgotten to take off his pyjamas. He flew downstairs again and got dressed in the smart new suit he had bought specially for the big day.

Ding-dong! chimed the doorbell. It was Finbarr's brother Davy, who was to be his best man. 'Finbarr,' he said, 'you're wearing one brown shoe and one black one. You're not wearing any socks and you've forgotten to do up the zip of your trousers. You have your shirt on back to front, you have your jacket on inside out, and you have the flower in your buttonhole upside-down.'

'Have I? Have I really? Ooh, thanks for telling me, Davy!'

Davy helped him to get himself sorted out, and in no time at all Finbarr looked quite splendid.

The church was packed with people. The whole town of Gillnacurry turned out because everybody was so fond of Finbarr and Emily. There were tall, skinny folk from Finbarr's family; and all of Emily's relatives were there, including Keira's mum and dad. But what made it a most remarkable wedding was that a great many of the guests were...animals.

Everybody was there from the shop – Mulvey, Bubbles, Noreen and Captain Cockle; the hamster, the kittens, the whole gang. Even the tank of tropical fish had been brought along and set on a pew near the front. Thanks to Presto ALL the mice were there, not just Willy and Billy and Milly and Tilly, but Fergal too, and even Fergal's brother Martin, the shy house mouse who lived behind the skirting board in the shop. Fergal and Martin hadn't seen each other for many years, and they had a joyous reunion. Davy had brought Nora and Nobby with him, Nora looking pretty with her fleece freshly washed and a lilac bow on her head. He had put a bow on Nobby too, but Nobby had eaten it on the way to the church.

Keira was a bridesmaid and wore a pink silk dress and shoes with ribbons, like a ballerina. Ryan was a pageboy and carried the rings on a velvet cushion. Emily had a crown of fresh flowers on her head, and a wonderful white dress covered in sequins and pearls. She also had a very long veil, and Nobby's eyes gleamed with hunger as he watched her walk up the aisle.

'Yum-bags scrum-bags!' he said.

'Just one nibble – just one – and I'll never speak to you ever again,' Nora hissed in his ear.

Finbarr thought his heart would burst with happiness and love as he watched Emily walk towards him. When they had made their vows and were married, everyone in the church shouted 'Hooray!' or squeaked or squawked or purred with delight. As they came out into the square afterwards, the two golden angels on the church tower chimed out a special tune, one no one had ever heard before, to celebrate the wedding of Emily and Finbarr.

The reception was a huge party with heaps of food for everyone. There was cake and champagne, ice-cream and chocolate. After a few glasses of champagne, some of the guests who had been a bit afraid of Noreen had the courage to touch her. 'Oh she's lovely and warm,' they cried. 'She's just like a handbag!'

Finbarr danced with Emily and Ryan danced with his mother. Davy danced with Nora the sheep and Mulvey danced with all the mice. It was that kind of wedding. Late in the evening, Henrietta danced with Finbarr. It has to be said, he wasn't exactly brilliant at the quickstep.

'You're standing on my toes, Finbarr.'

'Am I? Ooh, sorry about that, Mrs Fysshe-Pye.'

'Why, you got it right!'

'Two y's, two e's two s's and a hyphen,' he said proudly.

'That's wonderful! But you must call me Henrietta.'

'I like the hat,' Finbarr said, as the music stopped and they walked over to the table where Ryan was sitting. Henrietta was wearing an elegant little round straw hat with a wisp of net over her eyes.

'Thank you very much! I'm glad you like it.'

'Funny though, it's quite small. I thought you'd be wearing an enormous, great big hat,' Finbarr confessed.

'Oh I'm finished with big things,' Henrietta said smiling. 'Never again. The very first thing I'm going to do tomorrow is see about selling the castle.'

'Really, Mummy?' cried Ryan in delight. She nodded.

'And I've seen the most delightful little cottage for sale that I'm going to buy instead. It'll be perfect for the two of us. Although it's small, I'm sure there'll be room for a few pets. What would you like, Ryan?'

He hardly dared speak. 'The white rabbit?' he said at last.

'Why not? I'm sure that in time I could get used to the way its nose twitches,' replied his mother, beaming. 'And what about the kittens? We could get them as well, and even if they do grow up into ginger toms, well, it won't be the end of the world.'

'Oh thank you, Mummy! Thank you so much! They're exactly the pets I've always wanted.'

Then Emily threw her bride's bouquet into the crowd, and everybody laughed when Nobby caught it and gobbled it up.

'Delicious!' he sighed.

By now the sky was dark blue and a fine silver moon had appeared. No one noticed when a small fluffy bird with pale feathers swooped onto the window-sill and peered down into the room with its eyes as yellow as topaz.

'The Amazonian Rainforest Parrot!' the baby owl cried in delight, as it caught sight of Captain Cockle. 'There he is! I've always wanted to at least catch a glimpse of him again. How well I remember helping all those animals back to their shop! Oh what a wonderful night that was!'

And what a wonderful night THIS was. When all the guests finally made their way home, long after the angels on the church had dinged XII for midnight, everyone agreed that it was the best, the most beautiful, the most delightful wedding that there had ever been in the town of Gillnacurry.

The End

And what of Snowdrop and Feathers? They broke out of the zoo within a week and have been living ever since quite happily in the forest near Gillnacurry. Sometimes people out for a walk catch a glimpse of them, but never tell anybody that they've just seen a giant budgie or an enormous cat. They don't want their friends to think they've gone bonkers.

Henrietta kept her word to Ryan. She sold the castle and bought a charming cottage, painted cream with a blue front door. Presto, Aloysius and Alexander went to live there too. The kittens have grown up to be the biggest, fattest, most gingery ginger toms you ever saw, with deep green eyes and strong white whiskers. And do you know what? Henrietta LOVES them! She also loves Presto, who sits on her knee of an evening, perfectly still except for his twitching nose, which Henrietta now thinks is a most endearing feature. The cottage is much more comfortable and cosy than the castle ever was, and Ryan and his mother just couldn't be happier.

The same is true of Finbarr and Emily. Keira still comes to visit, not just in the summer now but at Christmas and Easter too, for there's so much to be done. There's not just the pet shop to be looked after, with all the animals, there are also the babies.

What babies?

Why, Finbarr and Emily's, of course! They had twins, a boy and a girl, the following year.

The little girl is plump and pretty and as sweet as her mother; and the little boy is a long, skinny baby with a dippy smile, the image of Finbarr. Keira loves them both to bits and is quite an expert at looking after them.

The pet shop is still going strong. Mulvey is there, with his basket and his tartan rug, Noreen is in her tank, Betty on her wheel – all of them, just as I've described them. Apart from Presto and the kittens, Emily has never sold any of the animals who had such extraordinary adventures over the course of that remarkable summer. Whenever anyone expresses an interest in buying one of them, Bubbles for example, or Captain Cockle, Emily always has the perfect explanation as to why they should stay exactly where they are.

And do you know what? I think she always will.

Orchard Red Apples

Utterly Me, Clarice Bean	Lauren Child	978 1 84362 304 5
Clarice Bean Spells Trouble	Lauren Child	978 1 84362 858 3
The Truth Cookie	Fiona Dunbar	978 1 84362 549 0*
Cupid Cakes	Fiona Dunbar	978 1 84362 688 6*
Chocolate Wishes	Fiona Dunbar	978 1 84362 689 3*
The Truth about Josie Green	Belinda Hollyer	978 1 84362 885 9
Hothouse Flower	Rose Impey	978 1 84616 215 2
Snakes' Elbows	Deirdre Madden	978 1 84362 640 4
43 Bin Street	Livi Michael	978 1 84362 725 8
Seventeen Times as High as the Moon	Livi Michael	978 1 84362 726 5
Do Not Read This Book	Pat Moon	978 1 84121 435 1
Do Not Read Any Further	Pat Moon	978 1 84121 456 6
Do Not Read – Or Else	Pat Moon	978 1 84616 082 0

All priced at £4.99 except those marked * which are £5.99

Orchard Red Apples are available from all good bookshops,
or can be ordered direct from the publisher:
Orchard Books, PO BOX 29, Douglas IM99 1BQ
Credit card orders please telephone 01624 836000
or fax 01624 837033
or visit our Internet site: www.wattspub.co.uk
or e-mail: bookshop@enterprise.net for details.

To order please quote title, author and ISBN
and your full name and address.
Cheques and postal orders should be made payable to 'Bookpost plc.'
Postage and packing is FREE within the UK
(overseas customers should add £1.00 per book).

Prices and availability are subject to change.